April North

LAWRENCE BLOCK
writing as Sheldon Lord

APRIL NORTH

LAWRENCE BLOCK writing as SHELDON LORD

A LAWRENCE BLOCK PRODUCTION

Classic Erotica

Classic Erotica #4

APRIL NORTH

Lawrence Block

Chapter 1

The town of Antrim is located in the south-central part of the state of Ohio midway between Cincinnati and Columbus. The population is either 4500 or 6500, depending upon whether you believe the U.S. Census Bureau or the Antrim Chamber of Commerce. Antrim also has a grammar school and high school, a small public library, one supermarket and four smaller food stores, one restaurant and five beaneries, one state liquor store and seven saloons.

The climate is typical for the area. The winter is always a little too cold, the summer a little too hot, and every spring and fall is a festival of rain. With the singular exception of Scherner Street, the town's main thoroughfare, all the streets of Antrim are peaceful and tree-shaded. The population explosion has not yet affected Antrim, which remains a *Main-Street* type of Midwestern small town.

The season was late October. The leaves had turned color and left the trees and small boys were earning extra money raking lawns. On the athletic field behind the high school, the team was going through after-school practice for the game coming up Saturday against Bryan High School of nearby Yellow Springs. Jeremy Keel was sweeping leaves and debris from the sidewalk in front of his barber shop into the Schwerner Street gutter. John

Parson was standing behind the counter in his food shop, wishing the supermarket would dry up and blow away so that his old customers might return to him. They were regular patrons when they needed credit but in these good times they could afford to pay cash at the supermarket.

The girl, carrying two books and a notebook under her arm, was walking north on Schwerner Street, away from the main business section. She was seventeen, five feet four, with sandy hair and hazel eyes. She had a good figure. Her young breasts, mature now after several painful adolescent years of boyish flatness, pushed out against the front of her yellow wool sweater. The Black Watch plaid skirt fell to a little below her knees and hugged hips that were already rounded. She wore thick white wool socks and brown-and-white saddle shoes.

Her name was April North.

She walked steadily and easily, with a fluid movement of her hips. Turning off Schwerner Street at Hayes Road, she headed toward the house where she lived with her mother, her father and her younger brother. Her mother was one of the leaders of the women's group at the Antrim Baptist Church, her father ran the more profitable of Antrim's two drugstores, and her brother Link was starting his sophomore year at Antrim High. But she was not thinking about her family as she walked. She was barely aware of where she was going and her feet moved more by instinct than design.

She was thinking about herself, April North. And she was thinking about Daniel Duncan. And—more than anything else—she was thinking about It.

She did not want to think about It. Somehow, It was not the

sort of thing you were supposed to think about, when you were a sweet and simple senior at Antrim High. Yet It was important and obviously a lot of people thought about It. She had read quite extensively about It, both in books she took from the public library and from the books her father sold in his drugstore. It was significant. It was important, but still, she did not want to think about It.

She could not seem to direct her mind onto another topic.

Because It had happened.

"Hey, April!"

She looked up. Two boys were tossing a football back and forth in the street. The one who called to her was gesturing as if to throw the football at her. She ducked and spun away automatically. Then she heard his laugh as he threw the football in a lazy spiral to the other boy. She recognized them vaguely as classmates of her brother Link.

"Scared you," the first one called out. "Must be thinking about something awful important."

She forced a laugh but they had already resumed their game and ignored her, and she went back to her walking and to her thinking. Suddenly she wished for a cigarette. She never smoked in public, certainly not on the street and hardly ever in her own home. But when she was out with Danny he would give her a cigarette and puffing it helped her relax. And now she wished she had a cigarette.

She could not escape the fact that It had happened.

Her thoughts drifted back to last Saturday night . . .

•   •   •

Saturday night was traditionally date night in Antrim, as it was in thousands of other towns from coast to coast. Couples who barely spoke to each other during the week went out every Saturday night for months in a row. Like most of the reasonably attractive girls in her class, April was going steady. Her steady was Dan Duncan, a tall, rangy senior who played first base on the baseball team and second-string end on the football team.

And, because it was Saturday night, they were out together. His father had let him use the family car for the night, a dark green Oldsmobile sedan a year old. This evening, April was sitting beside him in the front seat as he headed the car away from town on Route 68. They were alone in the car. Usually they double-dated with another couple, but tonight they were alone.

"We could go to the movies," he suggested. His tone seemed to indicate that he was not too keen on the idea.

"What's playing?"

"A western, I guess—*Sound of Distant Drums.* Something like that."

"Sounds lousy."

He nodded. "Not much else to do in this town," he said. "Go to a show or sit around the drugstore sipping a soda. No way to get excited about things."

She said nothing. She had a feeling she knew what he was leading up to, so she was not particularly surprised when he turned off onto the winding dirt road called Cemetery Hill Road. This was rather strange because the road ran along flat land devoid of cemeteries. Pretty soon, she thought, he would kill the motor and park the car.

For almost two months they had been in the habit of parking

at the conclusion of a date. At first they had simply exchanged a few kisses, then called it quits. Lately Danny had grown bolder, and his caresses had had a more pronounced effect upon her. There were times when, after he had dropped her at her home with a final good-night kiss, she had had great trouble falling asleep.

And now the date was going to begin on Cemetery Hill Road. This marked a significant change in their relationship, she knew. And if she permitted him to park now, she would be giving up leverage in a battle designed to deprive her of her virginity.

But she wanted him to park the car.

Inevitably he turned the ignition key and stilled the engine. Then he guided the car, coasting off the narrow road and into the high grasses at the side. He switched off the headlights then abruptly reached for her. There was a painfully awkward moment during which the situation seemed to have been staged and blocked out by an inept director on his first Broadway assignment. Then she was in his arms, her face snuggled tight against his chest, and everything was as it ought to be.

"April—"

She looked up and he took her face between his strong hands, bringing her mouth up to his. She wore no makeup, only a dab of lipstick on her lips. He kissed her and ground his mouth against hers. She felt desire build within her at a frightening pace. Her heart was beating faster than it should, her palms were moist.

He kissed her again. This time his tongue slid between her slightly parted lips and probed inside her mouth. He had done this before. At first it had seemed silly, laughable. Now it was stimulating.

His arms were around her and his hands rubbed the back of her sweater. Her whole body was miraculously alive with a new force she had never felt before. He kissed her again and this time her tongue seized the initiative, plunging into his mouth and savoring the warm male taste of him.

The kissing went on for a long time. There were moments when she was lost completely, forgetting who she was or where she was, aware only of what she was doing and how good it was to kiss like this. Finally he released her. They separated slowly, moving like creatures in a dream, and he took a crushed pack of cigarettes from his shirt pocket. He gave her one and took one for himself and lit them with the dashboard lighter.

She drew the smoke into her lungs and fought off the inevitable impulse to cough. Instead she blew the smoke out in a long thin column and watched it hover in the air of the closed car. Then Dan rolled down the window and the smoke trailed out into the darkness.

"Beautiful night," he said.

She nodded without speaking.

"This is nice," he went on. "Being here with you. Just relaxing and enjoying ourselves."

She was glad he had said that. His words seemed to excuse their presence there, to transform a trite petting situation into something reasonable and defensible. They smoked in silence and she listened to crickets chirp in the tall grass. There was a way to tell the temperature from the crickets. You counted the number of chirps in fourteen seconds, added forty, and the result was the temperature in degrees Fahrenheit. She considered asking Dan for his watch so that she could find out how warm it was. The thought was quietly ridiculous and she started to giggle.

"What's so funny?"

"Nothing. I was just thinking."

"What about?"

"I don't know. Something just struck me as funny. It's nothing important."

He took her cigarette from her and pitched it with his own out the window onto the road. She wondered if the cigarettes would start a fire. Then her thoughts were cut off because he was kissing her again.

She gasped. This time his clever hand had found her breast and he was holding her gently but firmly while his tongue darted into her mouth. His hand moved skillfully and her breast seemed alive and on fire. She could feel the outlines of his fingers as he stroked her and caressed her.

He had touched her breasts before, had touched them through her clothing, but this was somehow different. Before, his caresses had been stimulating but not intoxicating, inspiring warmth but not passion. But this was not the same now. This was passion, the first genuine passion she had ever felt.

She knew that she ought to stop him or at least make some pretense of resisting. But if she stopped him the warm feeling would go away and she did not want to lose it, did not want the sweet sensation of his hand upon her breast to cease. It was too good, too pleasant.

"April—"

And she murmured in reply: "Don't stop, Danny. It feels so good. Don't stop."

He took her at her word.

Her sweater was a long-sleeved cardigan that buttoned down in front. He released her and began to undo the buttons. This, she knew, was clearly wrong. A nice girl did not let a boy take her clothes off. Some girls, of course, were all too willing to let a boy undress them and do other things. But a great gulf separated these girls from nice girls like herself. Boys took these girls for rides, took their clothes off, make love to them. But boys married and respected nice girls.

He unbuttoned the last button and thrust his hand inside her sweater. She felt the teasing fingers on her breast. Only the thin white bra stood between those fingers and her bare flesh.

And she forgot all about nice girls.

"April—"

She looked at him.

"We oughta get in the back seat. There's more room back there."

"Maybe we shouldn't."

He shrugged. "Might as well be comfortable," he said. "It's not too comfortable here—the steering wheel, and everything. The back seat's better."

It was, she decided, quite a night for firsts. It was the first time he had parked right away on a date, and the first he had unbuttoned her sweater. Now it was the first time they had ever left the front seat for the back. The back seat, she knew, was where people did It. In the back seat they went All The Way. But she told herself that they were not going to go All The Way. It was just as Danny said—the back seat would be more comfortable to neck in, so why not use it?

They got into the back seat.

Immediately he kissed her again and his hand found its place inside her sweater. His other hand joined it, and both hands went around her body until they found the clasp of her bra. Again she felt that another milestone was being reached, but again she was unable to offer so much as token resistance. His fingers were clumsy, but he managed nevertheless to unlock the bra and remove it, leaving her firm breasts bare.

His hands fondled them.

"They're so pretty, April. So nice and firm. Do you like it when I touch them like this?"

She liked it much too much. Her whole body was throbbing with passion now and her breasts were quivering under his touch. Her nipples stood up stiff and alert, and every time his fingers brushed over them a jolt of pure passion went through her, spreading outward from her breasts and engulfing her entire body.

Then his fingers were on the hem of her skirt. He raised her skirt, slipped a hand under the cloth and squeezed her knee. This, she knew, was dangerous. They were treading on thin ice. When he had unbuttoned her sweater they had passed the thin and arbitrary line which distinguishes necking from petting. Now, with the new twist which he was adding by slipping his hand below her skirt, they were traversing another emotional boundary. There was a distinct difference between petting above the waist and petting below the waist. Even nice girls might pet above the waist with their steadies.

But below the waist was something different.

"We'd better stop." Her voice was only a whisper, and if he

heard it he paid no attention. Somehow she could not bring herself to repeat her mild protest. If what they were doing was wrong, why in the world did it feel so good? If it was indecent to let a boy touch your thighs, then why did it make them tingle so nicely?

A good question.

"So smooth," he was saying now, his tone reverent. "You've got the smoothest skin. So nice to touch."

It was only a matter of time before her panties were down and he was touching her more and she was quivering like a shimmering bowlful of jelly. It was only a matter of time before she was lying on her back on the car seat with her knees up and her brain swimming in equal parts of lust and fear. It was only a matter of time before he was crouching above her, ready for her.

"No!"

But again he ignored her, and again she did not have the strength to repeat herself. She knew inwardly that It was going to happen and that she wanted It as much as he did. She knew that It might very well be wrong, but that right or wrong It was going to take place.

She watched what he was doing, and she wondered whether he had had sense enough to visit her father's drugstore, or any drugstore. The thought almost made her laugh and then he was touching her again, and she was beyond laughter and beyond tears, ready for whatever would happen.

Then it began.

There was pain first, sheer pain that tore her in two and made her want to scream out against the night. The pain went all through her—she could not see or think or feel anything but all-consuming hurting.

But then the pain began to subside. And, magically, something else took the place of the pain. The pain gave way to a tide of pleasure greater than anything she had ever been able to imagine, a tide of pleasure that caught her up and spun her in whirling dizzying circles of light and darkness.

Magic.

Right or wrong, good or bad, clever or foolish—adjectives fell away from her, fell away before the advance of the tidal wave of pleasure. She let herself respond to the fullest, let her body move as it had to move and writhe as it had to writhe. The passion spun her around and raced forward with her and the world began to move with her and It was happening, happening, and nothing on earth could stop It.

It got better, and even better, and she felt his hot breath on her face and the heavy pressure of his strong young body upon her.

Then passion reached its peak. Then the tide of pleasure reached its crest and broke, and she held him in her arms and wept quietly into the night.

She was almost home. She thought about that night, about the way neither of them could speak when they had finished, about the way they sat together in the car and smoked two more cigarettes apiece before he drove her home. They did not stop for a soda at the Pink Pig as they usually did. And when he kissed her goodnight at her door there was something awkward about his kiss.

She had been unable to fall asleep for hours. She tossed and turned in her bed, worrying and frightened that she had done something wrong. Then she decided that everything would be all right. She would keep going out with Danny, and It would not happen again, and finally some day they would get married and live together and do It all the time. To do It when they were married would be all right. She did not know why this was, but that was the way things were supposed to be.

So they would be married, and everything would be all right.

But things were not working out that way. She had not seen him or heard from him on Sunday, and Monday in school he had passed her without speaking as if there were something wrong with her. She failed to understand and wanted to catch his arm and ask him what was the matter, but she realized dimly that it was his place to speak, and that she should wait for him to say something.

He said nothing.

He seemed to avoid her purposefully. There was nothing she could put her finger on but somehow he never spoke to her, never again met her in the hallway, and never called her on the phone.

Now it was Thursday afternoon. She did not even know if they were supposed to be going out Saturday night, and she did not see how she could ask him. She felt that she must have done something terribly wrong but could not figure out what her apparent error had been. She had only let him do what he wanted to do. Why should he be mad at her for that?

She reached her house. The lawn was still smooth and green, the leaves raked into a neat pile in the gutter. Soon the grass would turn brown and die for the winter, but for the time being it was fresh and green and beautiful. She walked up the flagstone path to the front door, opened it and went inside.

She studied until it was time for dinner. She did her advanced algebra homework, started the required reading for French III. When her mother called her for dinner, she went downstairs to the dining room for the evening meal. Her father talked about politics, and her brother talked about the football team, and her mother talked about a hand of bridge that had been badly misplayed by her partner that afternoon. April listened without hearing and ate in silence without tasting her food. She finished a piece of pie and a glass of milk for dessert and left the table.

At seven-thirty the phone rang.

Link answered. April barely heard the phone, concentrating at the time upon the remainder of the French, and she was surprised when her brother called her name.

"For you, April."

She left her room and walked to the phone. "It's a boy," Link added.

Was it Danny?

She took the receiver and held it to her ear. She said hello and waited.

"April?"

"This is April."

"Yeah. Well, this is Bill Piersall."

He was a tall, thin boy with a blond crew-cut. She did not know him too well.

"I was wondering if we could take in a show Saturday night. You and me."

That was a surprise. "I'm sorry," she said. "I'd like to go but I'm going steady. With Dan Duncan."

There was a pause.

"That's funny," Bill Piersall said.

"It is?"

"Yeah."

She waited.

"Danny told me to call you," the voice went on. "He said he isn't goin' steady with you any more. Said I ought to take you out."

Her mouth dropped open.

The voice went on, and now she could hear the smile in it. "He said I'd have a good time with you, April. Said you're pretty hot stuff. What do you say?"

Chapter 2

He said I'd have a good time with you, April. Said you're pretty hot stuff. What about it?

She was numb from head to foot. She moved in slow motion, replacing the receiver on the hook, turning from the phone and walking to the staircase. She went upstairs to her room and closed the door.

What do you say?

Well, what *do* you say? What do you think or feel? What do you do next?

She threw herself onto the bed and buried her face in the pillow. At first she thought she was going to cry, and she was surprised when no tears came. Finally she rolled over onto her back and stared up at the ceiling. She breathed deeply, trying to relax, trying to think straight.

Obviously, good old Danny had had a talk with good old Bill. And just as obviously, she had been the subject of their conversation. That much was easy to understand. The thing she was unable to figure out was why Danny would do a thing like that. It made no sense—just no sense at all.

For a short time she had been convinced that Danny loved her, that he was going to marry her. This somehow seemed not too likely any more. But why? Did he hate her because she had done what he had wanted her to do? Had he stopped respecting her when she had let him do It to her?

She nodded thoughtfully. That made some sense. That was what was in the books sometimes, and since the books were her only previous experience in this particular area, she had no choice but to accept what they told her. Obviously, Danny felt that she was no longer a nice girl, and therefore wanted nothing more to do with her. From there it followed that he would spread the word to his buddies so they could share his good luck.

Her reputation was made. She was a girl who put out, and as such she would be much in demand. It seemed only logical to assume that Danny would tell his best friends first. Since Bill Piersall was not a good friend of Danny's there were probably a lot of guys who had heard the word before him. So the word was out about April North. Everybody knew about her.

Ya hear about April North? Yeah, Danny Duncan gave it to her in the back seat. He says she's the hottest thing since canned heat. Lays like a rug. I figure I'll give her a try one of these days. She's not bad to look at. Hell, I wouldn't kick her out of bed or anything. I'm not one to turn down a sure piece . . .

From that point the course of events was clear. No boy would take her out because he thought he might like her company. What dates she had would be dates arranged with the object of getting her into an automobile's back seat in the shortest possible time. Even if she never let anybody else go All The Way with her, she would still be considered a not-nice girl, a girl who put out. And she would be treated accordingly.

Her mind swam. Her previous plans for the future, while pleasantly vague, had taken a certain form. She would graduate in June. In September she would enter Ohio State University as a freshman. Admission to OSU was automatic for any Ohio high school graduate. She would be admitted, she would do well, and she would not bust out during her freshman year as half the entering students did each year.

At college she would major in English. She would join a sorority, do a lot of dating, eventually get pinned and engaged and married to someone more or less like Dan Duncan. She would settle down, either in Antrim or in a town quite like it, be a housewife and raise children.

Plans.

They would no longer work that way. Her new-found reputation would make life in Antrim relatively impossible. Living through the few months between now and June would be difficult enough. Then her reputation would follow her to Ohio State and it would be the same thing all over again.

She wondered if she would go to college. She even wondered if she would manage to graduate from Antrim High. And, while she wondered, she was amazed at the very calm way she thought about these things. It was as if nothing mattered at all—no, it was more as though she had everything strangely under control. Her own calmness nearly frightened her. Maybe it was the calm before the storm. Maybe she was going to crack up any minute now and go all to pieces. But she did not think so.

Maybe—

"April!"

She walked to her bedroom door, opened it. It was her mother calling her this time.

"Telephone, April."

She walked slowly downstairs to the telephone. "It's a boy," her mother confided, handing her the telephone receiver. She took it, said hello to the mouthpiece, and waited.

"This is Jim Bregger, April."

"Oh," she said. "Hello, Jim."

"I just thought I'd give you a ring," he said. "Find out of you're free Friday night."

For a moment she thought of telling him that she was not free, that she was expensive. She almost came close to giggling, but she restrained the impulse.

"Friday," she said thoughtfully. "That's tomorrow night, isn't it?"

That's right."

"Well," she said, "how come you happened to call?"

"I thought maybe we could go out together," he said, sounding defensive. "That's all. Just thought we could go for a ride or take in a show or something."

"Oh," she said.

"Is it a date?"

"Well—"

"It's a date," he said. "Tomorrow night. I'll pick you up about eight or so, okay? We'll go for a ride or take in a show, something like that. I'll see you, April."

He hung up and she was left holding on to a dead phone. This annoyed her. She had never told him she would go out with him. As a matter of fact, she had been looking around for a polite way to tell him to go to hell, and now she was stuck with a date. And the date was one which he thought would lead to a quick tussle in the back seat of his father's car.

She did not want this to happen. She was about as interested in Jim Bregger as she was in swimming in boiling oil. He was fat, had pimples on his forehead and he was stupid.

And, according to him, he was going to make love to her tomorrow night.

She put the phone back on the hook. She walked into the living room and swiped two cigarettes from the tray on the coffee table. She picked up a pack of matches. Then she got her corduroy jacket from the back hall and put it on, slipping the cigarettes and the matches into a pocket.

"I'm going for a walk, Mom," she called. "I'll be back in a little while."

"Where are you going?"

"Nowhere special. Be back soon."

The air outside was brisk. She buttoned her jacket and walked along Hayes Road. The small street was empty of people, which was not surprising. The residents of Antrim seldom walked around after dinner. They either stayed at home or drove downtown to the movies or tavern. She turned off Hayes Road and into another side street. She fished into her pocket and took out one of the cigarettes. This was a little crumpled but she straightened it out and put it between her lips. She lit two matches, which the wind blew out, then got the cigarette going with a third. She took a puff and dragged smoke deep into her lungs. She blew out a cloud and felt better instantly.

Nice girls did not smoke on the street.

Nice girls did not go All The Way with boys.

She was not a nice girl.

Throughout the town of Antrim, the word was passing from

boy to boy that April North was a girl who could be made, a girl who had been there. Already it was relatively common knowledge that on Saturday night last, one April North did have sexual relations with one Daniel Duncan in said Duncan's automobile.

So it seemed a little silly to pass up a cigarette.

She noticed it in school the next day.

She noticed it instantly, and she began to wonder how she had missed it for the past four days. Now, knowing that Danny had turned informer, it was obvious. Boys gave her knowing looks. Girls looked at her thoughtfully, as if trying to discover what it had been like, how it might have changed her. There was a strange sort of distance in everyone's attitude—something she had missed on Monday and Tuesday and Wednesday and Thursday, but something which fit into place perfectly on Friday.

Jim Bregger gave her a solemn but knowing wink in the lunchroom, a wink that said he was going to show her one hell of a good time that night. A boy named Ralph Margate brushed up against her in the hallway between her sixth and seventh hour classes. She might not have noticed the maneuver a day earlier but now it was unmistakable. His hand rubbed her backside briefly and his hip bumped too-familiarly into hers.

When the bell rang she dropped off her books at her locker. The Greene County Bank and Savings Company stayed open until six o'clock on Fridays. She went directly to the bank, took her bankbook from her purse and presented it to the teller.

"A deposit, April?"

"A withdrawal," she said, hoping she sounded properly casual. "I want to take it all out."

"All of it?"

"That's right."

The teller, a gray-haired woman with thick glasses, frowned disapprovingly. In her weak eyes, thrift rivaled cleanliness for next place to godliness.

April explained. "I've been saving up for something," she said. "Now I've got enough money."

The teller's expression softened. She made the notation in the bank book and solemnly counted out five hundred and forty-five dollars and seventy-four cents. She presented the pile of bills and change to April.

"Lots of money," the teller said. "Sure you're not planning on running away from home, now?"

April managed to laugh. She scooped the money into her purse and fastened the clasp. Then, nonchalant as ever, she left the bank and headed for home.

On the sidewalk a boy fell into step beside her. "Hey, April," he said. "What do you say we stop for a soda?"

She looked at him. It was Bill Piersall, the boy who had been the first to call last night, the boy who had tipped her off to her present position in the Antrim social scale. Her first reaction was to tell him to take a flying jump in the nearest lake. Then she changed her mind. If he wanted to buy her a soda, she might as well take him up on it. It would hurt nothing. And she might find out something.

"Sure," she said. "Sounds good."

They crossed the street in the middle of the block, since

jaywalking was not a particularly hazardous sport in Antrim. They went to the drugstore—not the one her father owned, because his store did not have a fountain—and took stools at the counter. There were a few other students from Antrim High in a corner booth, but most of the Antrim High kids patronized the Sweet Shoppe for after-school eating.

"About last night," Bill said.

The waitress came, a tired-looking woman in her mid-thirties with massive circles under her eyes. Bill ordered a strawberry soda and April asked for a black-and-white sundae. The waitress went to make them.

"About last night," he said again. "On the phone."

She didn't say anything.

"I was kinda stupid. The way I talked, I mean. It wasn't too nice, I guess."

He had made a shrewd guess.

"I shouldn't have said it the way I did. But you know what I mean. I mean, it's not like you're a virgin or anything. You know what it's all about."

For a small moment she considered slapping his face, denying that she and Danny had done anything at all and running out of the store.

She considered this course of action dispassionately and rejected it just as dispassionately, knowing very well that such a thing would not do the least bit of good. The rumor was past denial now, and had assumed the character of a fact, accepted as such by the bulk of the high school community. There was no point trying to nip such a story in the bud—not when it was already in full bloom.

So she did not say anything.

"Just so we understand each other," he said. "So we know where we sit. I don't want you to be mad at me or anything. That would be silly."

The waitress, hollow-eyed and sad, returned with their orders. She set a pink frothy concoction in front of Bill and put a dish of vanilla ice cream topped with chocolate sauce on the counter in front of April. She gave April a spoon and Bill a straw. Bill gave her a half dollar and she went away again.

April took a bite of her sundae. It was cold and sweet and all a sundae should be. She ate several bites in silence.

"Sundae okay?"

"Fine," she said.

"They make 'em better here than at the Sweet Shoppe. More for your money."

And you can talk to a not-nice girl without your friends around, she added mentally. *You can make your play without any of the crowd watching . . .*

She ate more of her sundae and the drugstore was silent except for the *slurp* of Bill finishing his soda. She could tell that the stage was set. And so she decided to contribute her own little bit to the play.

"Can I have a cigarette?"

He looked at her for a second. Then he gave her a cigarette and lit it for her. It was a small enough act and the chances were great that nobody would notice it, but it set things up for Billy-boy. The coast was clear.

"April—"

She looked at him.

"Look, we know where we stand. You like it and I like it. So why shouldn't we get what we want?"

She flicked her ashes from her cigarette into the glass ashtray on the counter. She didn't say anything.

"You know what I mean," he whispered. "We'll take a little walk. A little walk in the woods, just the two of us. A walk in the fresh air. It's healthy."

"Now?"

"Sure."

"Now? In the middle of the afternoon?"

He shrugged. "No time like the present."

She wanted to laugh but something kept her from laughing. Why not? Why not take a little walk in the woods, just for the pure, sheer hell of it? It might even be fun. And it couldn't hurt anything. She was already a bad girl. She might as well have all the fun she could.

So she stood up and took his arm. "Why not?" she said. "A little walk won't hurt. And I like to walk in the woods. It's nice there."

As nice as a car, she thought.

The woods stood brave and silent on the north edge of town. Somehow a little over a hundred acres of wooded land had been ignored by progress and by Antrim. The area was not primeval cover; bushes and shrubs were thick, and the trees that grew there, mainly oaks were no more than thirty years old.

Leaves rumpled under their feet. The air was crisp, cool, fresh. The few birds that had not yet gone south for the winter sang foolishly in the branches.

They found a quiet spot and sat down.

Your cue, she thought.

And he came in right on cue. His arm went around her and his mouth went to her ear.

"You're a beautiful girl," he told her. "Really beautiful. And sweet. I like you very much, April."

That was funny. Why did he tell her these things? She could not have cared less whether he liked her or not, whether he thought she was beautiful or not. Saying these things would not help him to get her to go All The Way.

He kissed her and she analyzed the kiss, being quite cold and clinical about the whole thing. He gave her breast a squeeze and again she was the keen analytical mind, the sexual scientist adding and subtracting and observing phenomena.

His hand went under her skirt and touched her. And she was surprised

She had expected the cold, analytical attitude to last throughout the whole procedure.

It did not.

Her response astounded her. The reaction was immediate and unexpected, a sharp charge of sensation that overwhelmed her. Automatically she felt herself stiffening with passion and pulled him close, her young body yearning for him.

At four-thirty on the dot she returned to her own house, her purse under one arm and all the leaves brushed from her skirt and sweater. She walked in the front door and called hello to whomever might be home. Everyone was out—Link was somewhere, Dad was at the drugstore, Mom was at another meeting.

She went upstairs, changed her clothes, got a small suitcase from the attic. She filled the suitcase with clothing then added most of the five-hundred-odd dollars she'd gotten from the bank. Purses, she knew, got snatched—presumably by purse-snatchers, she guessed. Her money would be safer in the suitcase.

Bill Piersall was going to be a celebrity, she thought. He'd managed to get to her, and she'd given him a time he probably would remember for quite a while. Now, when she suddenly dropped out of the picture, he would be able to give everybody the last word on April North. This would bring great honor upon his head, by all the rules.

And Jim Bregger was the goat. She could just see his face when he turned up at eight o'clock and found out she was gone. He would be burning, all right—two hours away from a shot at April North, the notorious April North who was nothing but a sex-hungry nymphomaniac, as everyone in Antrim plainly knew.

And she could hear the ribbing he would take:

Man, if it wasn't for you she'd still be around. Why, she had a fling with Piersall and it was great, see. And then she thought of having to do it with you and it was too much of her. She couldn't stand it, Jimbo. So she cut out. You ruined it for everybody, Jimbo. Why, we all could have cut ourselves a piece of the cake, there was plenty to go around. But you had to louse it all up.

She laughed.

She snapped the suitcase shut and carried it downstairs. Her purse was slung over her other arm. Nobody saw her when she left the house, and no one saw her walking down Schwerner Street to the edge of town where it became Route 68. There was the place where the bus stopped, and a bus would be along soon. The bus would carry her to Xenia, where the Pennsy stopped on the way to New York.

She stood at the bus stop. After a few minutes she fumbled in her purse for a cigarette. She was kissing the town goodbye, and the old injunction against smoking in public hardly seemed to apply to her. She found a cigarette, put it in her mouth and lit it with the third match she scratched. The wind put the first two out, but on the third try the flame held and she drew smoke into her lungs. She shook the match out, threw it away, closed her purse, and let out a stream of smoke.

To hell with Antrim, she thought. To hell with the whole crowd of narrow-minded bastards. To hell with all of them. They could ruin her reputation but they could not ruin her. She would leave them. She would go to New York, where nobody knew her, and she would do whatever she damn well wanted to do. They could take this town and stick it, as far as she was concerned.

She shifted her weight from one foot to the other. She was slightly nervous now. Suppose someone should pass her while she was waiting for the bus? She was hardly standing in an inaccessible spot. Route 68 was simply an extension of Antrim's main thoroughfare, and anybody could pass by now and see her there. Suppose a relative came by—what could she do?

She would just have to work it out, she thought. She could tell him she had to take a run into Xenia to buy a book for school, something like that. And by the time her parents found out her lie their knowledge would do them no good. By then she would be on the train for New York and they would not be able to find her.

She barely noticed the sports car. She was lost in thought and hardly looked up when it churned by, heading into Antrim. But she did look up when brakes squealed and whined. She saw the sleek foreign car spin around in its tracks, making a sharp U-turn and pulling to a stop in front of her.

She stared at the driver.

He was no one she had seen before. If she had seen him, she would certainly have remembered him. He looked vastly different from the sort of people she was used to.

His hair was long and jet black. He had combed it lazily back over his head. His skin was deeply tanned, his features sharp and distinctive. His black mustache was neatly trimmed—it gave him a rakish look.

But his eyes were the main feature, as far as she was concerned. No eyes had ever looked at her with that combination of tacit approval and total self-assurance. It would not be quite accurate to say that his eyes undressed her. It was more that they probed beneath her skin.

"I see you're going my way," he said lazily. "Hop in, girl."

CHAPTER 3

For a long moment she could only stand, stunned. She watched as he leaned easily across the front seat to open the door for her. The door swung free and she looked at the open door, at the empty bucket seat, and at the man who was still eyeing her appreciatively.

"Get in," he said. "I won't bite. Not unless you want me to, at any rate."

"I was going to Xenia," she said finally.

"I'll drive you there."

"I was waiting for the bus."

"The bus costs forty cents," he said agreeably. "I don't have a meter in this thing yet, so I'll drive you free of charge. Besides, I drive much faster than buses."

"But—"

"Hop in, girl."

"Where do I put my suitcase?"

"On your pretty dimpled knees," he said. "Come on."

She seemed to have no will of her own. Automatically she climbed into the car, sat in the comfortable bucket seat, propped her suitcase up on her lap and closed the door. The man behind the wheel slammed the sports car into gear, let out the clutch and put the accelerator on the floor. The car leaped forward and she felt herself thrown forcibly against the back of her seat. The car picked up speed and the wind played with her hair, tossing it around recklessly.

She wondered who he was, where he lived, how old he might be. He was obviously several years older than the crowd she went around with, probably in his early or middle twenties, yet there was a distinctly youthful air about him. Well, she thought, it really didn't matter. He was giving her a ride to Xenia and that was all. She would probably never see him again.

"You're going to Xenia," he said. "Right?"

"That's right."

"Why? What's in Xenia?"

"A railroad station."

"Going on a trip?"

"To New York."

He nodded slowly. "When will you be back?"

She didn't even think of lying to him. "I won't be back," she said. "I'm going to stay in New York."

"Why?"

Was he going to ask her questions forever? "Because I don't like Antrim."

"God above. Does anybody like Antrim?"

"Some people may."

"So you're running away from home. That's what it amounts to, isn't it?"

"I suppose so."

"God above," he said again. He turned to look at her and she avoided the intensity of his gaze. "What's your name, girl?"

"April."

"Is that all?"

"April North."

"April North," he repeated. "A good name. I like it."

"Thanks. I'll keep it."

He laughed, loud clear laughter that rang above the throbbing of the car's engine. When he turned to look at her again she felt his eyes rubbing over her breasts like friendly hands. Her breathing speeded up and her hands trembled in her lap. She had never felt like this before. Just by looking at her he could set her nerves on edge.

And she did not even know his name.

Abruptly he swung the wheel, pulling the sports car off onto an asphalt road. He pressed harder on the accelerator and the car took up the challenge, racing along the black pavement like an angry demon. She saw the speedometer needle hover for an instant at eighty, move onward past ninety, close to one hundred. She had never gone so fast before. The thought occurred to her that she ought to be frightened, but somehow she was not scared at all. She felt intuitively that he knew what he was doing, that he was a good driver and nothing would happen to them.

She said, "This isn't the way to Xenia."

"It's a short cut."

She knew he was lying but did not want to argue with him. She leaned back in her seat, enjoying the ride, abandoning herself to the tug of the wind at her hair and the excitement of speed. The low-slung car hugged the ground—this was far more exciting than riding in a regular car, far more exhilarating. She looked at his hands on the wheel, saw how he concentrated on the act of driving with all his being. It was as though he and the car were two parts of a single mechanism, she thought.

When he turned from the asphalt road and onto a gravel road, she knew beyond any possible doubt that they were not going to Xenia. He was probably going to take her somewhere in the country and seduce her, she decided. Maybe he would rape her if she refused, or else toss her out of the car to walk home. Well, he had no need to worry. She would give in, if that was what he wanted. If she could give in to Bill Piersall, she could just as easily give in to this man. At least he looked as if he had a better idea of what to do than Bill did.

Besides, she admitted, she was excited. Evidently the boys in Antrim were right, because she was excited and ready for sex. It was ridiculous—she didn't even know this man. But she knew that she would do whatever he wanted her to do.

The car stopped with a screech of rubber. "We're here," he announced. "Get out of the car, April."

"Where are we?"

"At my house. Do you like it?"

She stared. The house was set back some fifty yards from the road at the peak of a sharp hill, and it was unlike any house she had ever seen in Antrim. The architectural style was dramatically contemporary, somewhat in the manner of Frank Lloyd Wright, and no one else in the area had a house remotely like it. April had seen similar homes in the movies and on television. But shoddy one-floor ranch homes were as close as Antrim permitted itself to come to the twentieth century.

This house was startlingly but pleasantly different. Sharp planes of brick and glass thrust themselves at odd angles. A circular courtyard made a mouth out of the house's front entrance. The landscaping was precisely suited to the house and strengthened the impression that the structure had grown from the ground itself.

"Well? Do you like it?"

"Yes," she said honestly. "I like it very much."

"It's my home," he said. "The architect who designed it was a classmate of mine at Chicago. Before I was thrown out, that is. I'm glad you like it."

"Do you live with your parents?"

"My parents are dead."

"Oh," she said. "I'm sorry."

"Don't be," he told her. "I'm not. I didn't like them. Come on inside, April."

On the flagstone path leading to the front door, she remembered for the first time that she had been on her way to Xenia. She mentioned this.

"I can't take you to Xenia," he said.

"Why not?"

"Because you're running away from home. Now if I helped you run away from home, I would be contributing to the delinquency of a minor. You can't expect me to do that, can you?"

"Then you should have let me take the bus."

"But then I didn't know you were running away. I want to talk to you, April. We'll sit in my living room and drink a drink or two and you'll tell me why you want to run away. That's all. Fair enough?"

"I don't know."

"You're being silly," he said. "Look, you've said that you like the house. Wouldn't you like to see how the inside looks?"

He did not wait for an answer. He took her suitcase in one hand and her arm in the other and led her to the door. He shouldered the door open and led her inside, closing the door after her. "There," he said. "Like it?"

The interior of the house matched the exterior in the sharpness of its contemporary lines. But April would not have believed that such an angular sort of house could seem so warm within. The floors were of highly polished wood, with high-piled rugs placed here and there across the huge living room. The furniture was wood and steel, the wood deeply-grained and the steel black and shiny. In the huge flagstone fireplace at one end of the living room logs were piled, ready for the iron lighter at one side.

"It's very nice," she said lamely.

"I'll get you a drink. Scotch all right?"

"I guess so."

"Have a seat, April."

She sat on a couch that turned out to be far more comfortable than it looked, while he went to the bar and poured drinks. He came back, stopping on his way to flick a switch on the wall. Music filtered into the room, coming, it seemed, from all sides. It was modern jazz, penetrating and insistent. He handed her a drink and sat beside her on the couch.

"I suppose you wonder who I am," he said.

"That's putting it mildly."

He laughed again. "My name is Craig," he said. "Craig Jeffers. I'm very rich, as you've probably guessed, and I'm very wild, as you've probably guessed, also. I live alone here. My parents lived in Dayton, where my father made an enormous amount of money. I'm not sure just how he made the money, although I suppose he made it by giving some poor slobs the wrong end of the stick. He was that sort of a bastard."

April said nothing.

"He's dead now," Craig went on dispassionately. "I'm not unhappy about it. He killed mother two years ago, then put a bullet through his own brain. You probably read about it. It even made the wire services and of course the local press had an absolute blast with it."

She remembered, dimly. Headlines had screamed, local industrialist kills self, wife. She nodded dutifully and took a sip of her drink. She was not used to straight liquor, but this was very smooth and she did not choke on it.

"That's the story of my life," he said. "What little there has been of it so far, at any rate. I'm twenty-six. I live here because I want to. I've been all over the United States and through most of Europe. I've watched bullfights in Spain and I've slept with Paris whores. I've raced cars in California and I've gambled in Miami. I live here, in this horrible section of the horrible state of Ohio."

"Why?"

"Because I want to, April. Because this is my home, perhaps. I have my house and I have my car. Do you like the car, by the way?"

"Yes."

"It's a Mercedes-Benz 300-SL. It handles like a dream and goes like hell. I like it too."

He tossed off the rest of his drink and set the empty glass on the coffee table. He took out a pack of cigarettes and gave one to her, keeping another for himself. He lighted both of them and they sat side by side smoking. She drank more of her drink. The liquor was making her feel pleasantly lightheaded. She sipped and smoked.

"That's my story," Craig said suddenly. "Now it's time for you to tell me yours."

"There's nothing to tell."

"Nothing?"

"I live with my parents and go to high school in Antrim. That's all there is to it."

He arched his eyebrows. "You were on your way to Xenia," he said. "From there you were going to take a train to New York, and you weren't coming back. Now don't try to tell me there's nothing more besides the fact that you live at home and go to high school in Antrim. You have to do better than that, April."

She stared into her glass of scotch, avoiding his eyes. Her story was not the kind you went around telling to people, she thought. But by the same token he was not the sort of person you usually ran across. And there was something about him that made her want to open up, something that somehow inspired her confidence.

"It's not a pretty story," she said.

"Few stories are. Not the interesting ones, at any rate."

"And I'm not as sweet and innocent as I seem."

"Well," he said, "thank God for that."

She laughed. The drink was working now, loosening her up, letting her unwind. And the music, the insistently pulsating jazz, was also working. She looked around the room, deciding that she felt at home here, that she was comfortable. She looked at

Craig and decided that he was the most exciting man she had ever met. She could not imagine why he would want to waste his time talking to her. He could have any girl in the world, she told herself. And he could do more than talk to them.

"All right," she said slowly. "I'll tell you."

When she had finished, he stood up from the couch, took her empty glass and carried it to the bar. He dropped two fresh ice cubes into the glass and added a healthy splash of scotch. He made a drink for himself, brought back the two glasses and gave her one.

"To the new April North," he said.

They touched glasses and she took a drink. She was somehow much calmer now. And glad that she had told him.

"April," he said, "if you run away to New York you're a silly damned fool."

"What do you mean?"

"Exactly what I just said. Don't you see what you'll be doing? You'll be accepting the judgment of this godforsaken little town, living by its values and tolerating its opinion of you. Antrim thinks you're a tramp. Right?"

"Right."

He sighed. "Do you think you'll change their minds by running away? Do you think you'll show much backbone by creeping out of town like a thief in the night? That won't stop them from talking about you, April. It will only reinforce their opinions. God, don't you see what a stupid thing you'll be doing?"

She stared at him. She had not thought of it that way at all. Running away had looked like the perfect solution to her. But now, listening to him, she saw that he was right. You could not change things by fleeing from them. You escaped everything but yourself.

"Then—what should I do?"

"Stay here."

"And sleep with every pimple-faced pig in the senior class? Is that an answer?"

"No," he said. "That's not an answer."

"Then—"

He sighed again. "April," he said, "you're a big girl now. You have managed to discover something that few girls realize in the course of their entire lives, and that very few come to realize while they are your age. You've found out that most people are narrow-minded fools and that their standards are absurd. Do you feel that you've done anything wrong?"

"I don't know."

Craig stared hard at her. Then his eyebrows went up a notch to mock her. "Don't you know? All you did was admit that you were a woman with the desires of a woman. You gave in, you let your desires express themselves. Does that constitute a sin?"

"No," she said.

"Then did you do anything wrong?"

"No."

He sighed. "If you run away," he said gently, "you'll be admitting that you've done something wrong. You'll be running away from Antrim and from the ideals of Antrim."

"Then what should I do?"

"Stay here."

"But I hate it here."

"Do you?" He grinned. "I thought you liked my house, April."

"I mean that I hate Antrim. And—"

"Stay here," he said firmly. "Stay in Antrim. But don't stay as a child—that's as bad as running away like a child. Grow up, April. Grow into yourself. You can't act like a little girl because you're not a little girl any longer. You've given up the right to be a little girl. You're a woman now."

He was silent. She sipped some of the scotch, thinking about what he had told her. Despite her earlier feelings, she knew that Craig Jeffers was right. She could not run away. To run was to give up, and to give up was wrong.

But how could she stay in Antrim? If she went on with the life she had been leading, she would only manage to serve as the butt of every off-color joke told in the Antrim High locker rooms until the day she graduated. The boys were absolutists, she knew. Give in to one of them and you were a tramp and nothing more. There were no shades of moralistic gray. Everything was either black or white.

"What can I do, Craig?"

He picked up his glass, swung it in a little circle so that the ice cubes bounced against one another. He took a quick sip of the scotch and put the glass down again. "You'll go on living at home," he said. "You'll continue to go to high school, unless they throw you out or something like that."

"And?"

"And you'll have nothing to do with the boys and girls in your classes. You'll cut them dead. They're just children, April. You don't need them."

It was so easy to say. "What will I do, then?"

"You'll be with me."

"With you?"

He stood up and began to walk across the room. He turned suddenly and held his arms out. "There's a whole wonderful world that you don't know a thing about," he said. "Do you think I'm the only person in the state of Ohio who knows how to live? I'm not, April. There are other men and women like me, mature people who've managed to grow up without getting stuffy. Fellows who drive fast cars and girls who have come to realize that a bed is more comfortable than the back seat of a car. April, you may not go to the senior prom, but I'll take you to parties that your friend Danny Duncan would give his left testicle to attend. You may not ride around in hotrods, but you'll find out what a 300-SL can do on a straight track. You won't drink warm beer at the beach—instead you'll get high on good scotch with soft music cooking in the background."

He took a breath. "I sound like a preacher describing heaven, don't I? Sometimes I get a bit carried away with myself, April. But I mean what I've said. You don't have to feel deprived because you can't be a baby any more. Instead you have to learn to be a woman."

"I don't know if I'm ready."

"You're ready."

She studied the floor. In a low voice she said, "I'm not very smart or sophisticated. I don't know the right things to say. Your friends would laugh at me."

"No one will laugh at you."

"Are you sure?"

"I'm sure. April, you're smarter than you think you are. And as far as sophistication goes, it's not something a person is born with. It's developed, when you're ready for it."

"And you think I'm ready?"

"I know you're ready."

She finished her drink. The liquor was working and she could feel its effects, yet she did not feel drunk at all. Instead it was as though the liquor made everything clearer and more vivid, as though she could see things now as they really were. Craig was right, she decided. He was absolutely right.

She stood up. Craig had a mustache, she thought. In Antrim only a few old men had mustaches—what was the matter with him. But Craig looked good with his, she knew. It made him look dashing and exciting. She decided that he was the only really exciting person she had ever met.

"April—"

She looked at him. He was standing straight as a ramrod now, his eyes beckoning to her. She walked over to him like a person in a hypnotic trance. Her whole body tingled with life. She moved closer, wishing he would take hold of her, and when his arms reached for her she threw herself against him, her heart racing.

He kissed her. His lips were tender at first, incredibly tender, and then he was holding her tightly and his tongue was a flaming sword that burned the inside of her mouth. She felt her breasts drawn hard against his chest, felt desire building up in her loins and spreading through her body like a raging forest fire. Her knees were shaking and she could barely breathe.

Suddenly he released her. She floundered for a moment, then regained her balance and stepped backward slightly. She wondered what he was going to do next.

He said, "You're sweet, April."

She was silent.

"Very sweet," he said. "Do you want to go to bed with me, April?"

She nodded.

"And I want to go to bed with you, April. But not now. To-morrow night, April. When we have all the time that we need."

He laughed. "Come on," he said. "I'm going to take you home, April."

She went with him.

Chapter 4

There was only one point where she felt foolish. All the way home, her neat buttocks cupped by the bucket seat of the low-slung Mercedes, her suitcase propped again upon her knees, everything seemed perfectly logical, perfectly free and easy. And when Craig leaned over lazily in front of her house to brush her lips with a fleeting kiss, everything was still quite perfect and quite sensible.

But when the Mercedes roared like a lion and headed back for Craig's home, and when she was left to enter her house alone, suitcase in hand, everything was not quite so perfect or logical or sensible any longer. Alone now, she was a little girl who had been trying to run away from home, and who was now returning with her suitcase in her hand and her tail between her legs. No matter how sensible her actions might be when viewed from a distance, here she was with her silly suitcase and there was her house, looming ominously at her, and there was just no way to get the suitcase into the house without looking like several different kinds of a damn fool. The hour was quarter to eight—she had missed dinner and she was getting home just in time to tell Jim Bregger that he could go to hell for himself because she was not going out with him, after all. Perhaps some people could have felt perfectly calm about coming home under such circumstances but April was not one of them, not by any means.

The front door was ajar. She gave it a shove and walked in, hoping that no one was home. But just as she stepped into the hall her mother materialized, dishcloth in hand and worried look in eyes.

"April—"

"I meant to call," she said, improvising furiously. "I tried once and the line was busy, and then it was time for dinner. And after dinner I figured it would be just as quick to come home as to call, so I didn't. Call, that is. I'm sorry, Mom."

"Where were you?"

"Judy Liverpool's house," she said. "I went over there after school and then they asked me to stay for dinner and I figured it would be all right."

"You should have called, April."

"I know," she said. She managed to remember the suitcase before her mother noticed it. "I was going to stay the night," she lied neatly. "But I changed my mind. Besides, I've got a date tonight and he's coming any minute, so I have to be home to tell him that I won't go out with him."

The words came too fast for Mrs. North—the sentences changed direction too chaotically and she was hopelessly lost. "A date," she said weakly. "And you aren't going?"

"No, Mom. It's with Jim Bregger, and he has a terrible reputation with the girls, only I didn't know about it when I made the date, but Judy Liverpool told me and I know about it now. So I'm not going."

"A bad reputation?"

April nodded slowly. "They say he tries to get girls to do things," she said. "You know what I mean, Mom."

Mrs. North could guess. "You're absolutely right," she said. "Don't you dare go out with him. I know you wouldn't let him do anything, April—"

"Of course not."

"—but you have to safeguard your own reputation, you know. When a girl dates a fast boy, even if she's completely innocent, folks begin to talk. You have to guard against that sort of talk, April. Evil tongues do the devil's work."

"Yes, Mom."

Mrs. North turned and carried her dishcloth back to the sink.

April scampered up the stairs, closed her door and unpacked her suitcase. Nice lying, she thought. Very smooth, although if Craig had heard her he might have revised his opinion of her maturity. Still, she had handled things well. The suitcase gambit had brushed by without parental notice, the missed dinner was forgotten and Jim Bregger no longer had a leg to stand on as far as Mrs. North was concerned.

Now all she had to do was get rid of Bregger and sit on her heels for a day until Craig picked her up. As soon as he did, everything was going to be roses. She knew that as well as she knew her own name.

Because Craig was something special. The difference between a man like Craig and boys like Danny Duncan and Bill Piersall was about the same as the difference between 1949 Beaujolais and the ninth pressing of last year's California grapes. Craig was a man, not a typical Antrim man who grew stolid and stupid the day he passed twenty-one, but a cosmopolitan type who actually matured and who actually remained young inside. Craig had drive and fire, and Craig appreciated her, and Craig—

She wondered if she was in love with him.

Probably, she decided. Love was a funny word, a tough thing to get hold of. For a stupid while she had imagined herself in love with Danny and as soon as she had shown her love for him he had decided to share her fair white body with the rest of the male half of the senior class. So she was not exactly sure what love was, or whether or not she was ready to think about it.

But she was fairly sure about Craig. She was sure that he knew more than she did, and that he had done more than she had, and that he could make her life worthwhile again. As he had said, she might not go for rides in hotrods any more but Craig's Mercedes could give Bill's rod cards and spades and leave it standing at the post. And she had a fair notion that Craig's parties could do the same for the senior prom.

Well, she was going to have fun now. Of course, Craig expected her to sleep with him, but this did not bother her. You cheapened yourself when you let a high-school boy sleep with you— you only turned yourself into a tramp. But when you slept with a man like Craig Jeffers it was part of being a mature individual in a sophisticated world. She would not feel cheap, not after an affair with Craig. She would feel like a woman.

She finished unpacking her suitcase and went downstairs again. Her father was in the living room, the evening paper in front of his face. He lowered the paper and smiled slightly at her. It was a typical central Ohio smile, she thought. Empty and meaningless and a little silly-looking.

"Hi," he said. "Ma said you ate over at the Liverpool's."

"That's right."

"Hungry? There's some roast left in the fridge."

"I had plenty to eat, Dad."

"Well," he said. "Have a seat, hon."

She sat down on the flowered couch and he returned to his newspaper. The same thing every night, she thought, with Mom doing dishes and Dad reading the paper. She wondered suddenly if they made love any more. For people that old still to have sex seemed to her somehow indecent. But to think that they might have just given it up seemed even worse.

How horrible to grow too old for it, she thought. Just to sit around and realize that most of life had already passed you by. She wondered just how old you were when you were too old for it. When did you stop wanting and needing it? And when did men stop wanting and needing you?

She tried to imagine her mother, walking alone down a street in another city. Suppose a man saw her, she thought. Would he give her that look? Would he want to have sex with her? Would he think she was still desirable? And what would her mother do if a man made a pass at her? And what would—

I'm being silly, she told herself. She crossed one leg over the other and looked idly at her knee. Did Craig think she had nice legs? Did Craig think she had a nice body?

She sighed. There was some roast beef in the refrigerator, and she was dying of hunger. But she could not go into the kitchen and start gnawing on the roast and still live up to the lie about the wonderful dinner she had just finished packing away at the Liverpool's. Well, it would not hurt her to miss a meal.

The doorbell rang.

She stood up. Her father had started to fold his newspaper,

but she shook her head and walked past him. "It's for me," she explained. "A boy."

"Got a date, hon?"

"Not exactly," she said.

When she opened the door, her not-exactly date stood on the stoop with a silly expression on his face. She tried to decide whether he was nervous or excited. It was hard to say.

"Jim—"

"April—"

They had both started talking at once, throwing their names at each other, and now they stopped at once. She looked at him for a second or two, taking him in from his oiled black hair to his scuffed brown loafers. Now, she thought, if she were going to start putting out for the fine young men of Antrim, she could not find a less exciting start than Jim Bregger. Admittedly, the FYM of Antrim were a moldy lot, but Jumping Jim Bregger was the bottom of the barrel.

He was fat. And he had pimples. He was not merely fat—he was jellyfish, with no discernible muscles. And he did not just have pimples—even his pimples had pimples. He was so thoroughly a mass of acne that, when you looked at him, you wanted to squeeze his head.

"April," he said, "I can't go out with you tonight."

That's right, she thought. You can't.

But how in the world did he know this fact already? She had not yet opened her mouth, except to spit his name at him.

"I'm sorry," he went on. "But I can't go out with you."

She asked him why he could not. It occurred to her that this was a little like examining the dentures of a gift horse but she just had to know. Maybe his mother would not let him go out with a horny little tramp like her. Maybe—

He said, "Bill Piersall told me."

Sure, she thought. First Danny Duncan told you, and then Bill Piersall told you. It figures.

"He said you're—well, his property now. He said he's dating you steady and everybody better lay off. Stay away, I mean. He said if I kept my date with you tonight he'd scramble my brains for me. That's what he said, April."

Jim Bregger's brains didn't need scrambling, April thought. They were already poached.

"Wait a minute," she said suddenly. "Bill told you—that I was his property?"

"That's what he said."

"You go tell him he can go to hell," she said. "You tell Bill Piersall I wouldn't spit on him if he was dying of thirst. You tell him—"

"You mean you're not going with him?"

"You're almost as clever as you are handsome," she told him. "No, I'm not going with Bill Piersall. Not even to a dog show. Not to a funeral. Not even to his own."

"But—"

"Bill Piersall," she said firmly, "can go to hell."

She looked at Jim. He was shifting his weight from one foot to another while he shifted his wad of chewing gum from one side of his mouth to the other. She wondered if he was testing his coordination or something.

"That means you want to go out with me," he said.

"Huh?"

"I guess it's okay then," he said. "I mean, if Bill was mistaken, what the hell? I mean, we can go out for a ride and park somewhere, and—"

"I'm not going out with you," she said.

"But—"

"Jim," she said, "I don't even like you."

He stood there with a stupid half-grin on his face until she closed the door. She went back to the living room, sat down once more on the flowered couch. Her father asked her if anything had gone wrong, and she told him nothing had. He went back to his newspaper and she put the television on.

There was nothing good on television. She sat in front of the set for an hour, hardly noticing the program, thinking instead about what Jim had told her. Except for the one small moment of triumph when she had insulted him rather magnificently, the little interlude in the doorway had not gone exactly as she had wished. The word about Bill, for example, was not the most exhilarating news in the world.

So Bill thought she belonged to him, did he? She had let herself belong to him, for a few small moments in a small bed of rumpled leaves, but that had been when she was sure she would never be seeing the bright lights of Antrim again. That had been as much a joke as anything else, and the fact that she had had a certain amount of fun with Bill had been nothing but an extra kick.

But now he thought he owned her. Now, evidently, he had taken the tumble to heart and wanted her for his one and only, to tumble when he so desired. Well, he was due for a rude awakening.

He could hop on his noisy hotrod and take a fast trip to hell for himself. She never wanted to see him again.

At nine-thirty she kissed her father and mother goodnight and went upstairs. She flicked on the radio, but the usual diet of rock-and-roll seemed pale in comparison with the subtle jazz Craig had played for her. The rock-and-roll was Danny's speed, or Bill's, or Jim Bregger's. Once it had been hers, but now she was swinging at a fast tempo. Now it took something a little more complex to get to her.

She sat on the edge of her bed, trying to find a good radio station somewhere on the band. The best she could do was hill-billy music, which was not a significant improvement over the rock-and-roll. She turned off the radio and listened to the silence.

It was golden.

Bedtime, she thought. Little girl, you've had a busy day. You emptied your savings account, gotten banged in the bushes, met a guy who swept you off both feet at once, and came home with your suitcase between your legs.

Which is plenty for one day.

Besides, she thought, she had to be fresh and wide awake tomorrow. Tomorrow Craig was coming for her, and she had an idea the evening would turn out to be one blazing hell of a time. A good night's sleep would not hurt.

She went to the bathroom, washed her face, brushed her teeth. Back in her own room, she undressed slowly, hanging her clothes in the closet. She closed the closet door and looked at herself in the mirror. She was still wearing her bra and panties, her shoes and socks.

She kicked off the shoes, rolled down the socks. She reached behind her, forcing her breasts into sharp relief as she drew her shoulders back. She unhooked her bra and dropped it to the floor.

Her breasts were large and perfectly formed. She studied them, remembering the way Craig had looked at them. But he had not really seen them, not as she was seeing them now. He had not put his hands on them and touched them and traced little circles around the ruby tips.

She sighed. She looked at herself, at her own hands gripping her own breasts, and in her mind they turned to Craig's hands, strong and possessive upon her. She toyed with her nipples until they stood erect and stiff, and she hefted the weight of her breasts, pleased with their perfectly formed fullness. Craig Jeffers, she knew, would like them. Craig would take off her bra to caress them, and Craig would lower his face to kiss them, and—

She shoved her panties down over her hips, past her thighs, until they lay bunched around her ankles. She stepped out of them and looked at herself, completely nude, needing only a man to make the picture complete—a big nude man, like Craig.

Her hands left her breasts and moved downward. She touched herself and her hands thrilled her. Tomorrow, a voice sang in her ear. Tomorrow night, in Craig's house, in Craig's bedroom and in Craig's arms.

She tossed for an hour before she fell asleep. For an hour her hands were Craig's hands, touching and fondling and exciting . . . Finally, she slept.

No one woke her in the morning for Saturday was a day of rest and on Saturday she had the right to get up when she wished. She awoke a few minutes after nine but she did not get up just then. Instead she remained snug in her warm bed for almost a

full hour, finally emerging from beneath the covers at a quarter
to ten. She yawned and stretched like a fat cat before an open
fire, feeling the tingling in her body as her arms and legs came to
life and prepared for a new day. She hurried down the hall to the
bathroom, showered and brushed her teeth, then returned to her
room and dressed.

It was a day to do nothing in and accordingly she dressed in an
old pair of dungarees and one of her brother's discarded flannel
shirts. She rubber-banded her soft brown hair into a pony tail,
put socks and saddle shoes on her feet, and went downstairs for
breakfast. Her father was at the drugstore and Link had gone off
somewhere with a football under his arm, but her mother was
still in the kitchen. She scrambled a pair of eggs for April and
poured her a glass of milk.

"Could I have coffee, Mom?"

"I didn't know you liked it. Something new?"

"Not new," she said a little defensively. "I just think I'm old
enough to drink coffee. That's all."

Mrs. North smiled. "Cream and sugar?"

"Black, please."

The coffee did not taste very good, and she wished she had
taken it with cream and sugar. Still, this was the best way to get
used to it. And once she was used to it she would probably learn
to like it, the way everybody else did.

"Did you have any trouble with that Bregger boy, April?"

"No trouble," she said. "I just told him I wouldn't go out with
him."

"That's the right way, April. Have you a date tonight?"

She only hesitated for a moment. "Yes," she said. "Yes, Mom, I do."

"With anybody I know?"

"I don't think you know him."

"Oh? Who is he, then?"

"Craig Jeffers."

Mrs. North pursed her lips thoughtfully. "No," she said, "I don't believe I do. He a boy in your class, April?"

"No, he's not."

"From Antrim?"

"No," she said. Then, "From Xenia." It was not true but it was as close as she could come to the truth. If she told her mother that Craig lived in a big modern house in the middle of the woods, the woman would think she was out of her mind. "From Xenia," she repeated lamely. "I met him a few days ago."

"A high-school boy?"

"No," she said. "No, he's older, Mom. A few years older than I am."

"In college?"

"I think he's through with college, Mom."

"Are you sure he's a nice boy, April?"

"Yes," she said with finality. "He's a very nice boy, Mother. I wouldn't go out with him otherwise."

She finished her coffee in silence, then went out in the back yard to get some sun. It was a good day for Antrim, the sun high and hot, the air clear, the sky cloudless, a gentle breeze blowing. She stretched out on the chaise and almost fell asleep again thinking about Craig.

At twelve her mother called her to the phone. It was Bill Piersall.

"I have to talk to you," April, he said. "Jim Bregger said you said something to him and I have to talk to you."

"I don't have to talk to you," she said angrily. She hung up on him.

He called back immediately. "April," he said, "just listen for a minute—"

She hung up on him again.

Ten minutes later she heard his car take the corner of Schwerner Street and gun up Hayes at top speed. There was no missing Bill's hotrod, a Model A Ford with a late-model Chrysler motor and a LaSalle transmission and Bill had built it himself. He was very proud of it—the rod could outdrag anything else in Antrim. As far as April was concerned, he could take the thing and drive it off a cliff.

She sighed, stood up and walked down the driveway to the front yard. She might as well talk to him, she thought. Otherwise he would only keep annoying her. This way she could get rid of him once and for all.

She got to the front yard just as he was piling out of the car. He hurried over to her, a strange expression on his face. "I don't get it," he said. "Damn it, I just don't get it."

"There's nothing much to get," she told him. "I don't want to have anything to do with you. Period. Isn't that simple enough for you to understand?"

He stared at her. She looked at him, mentally comparing him

with Craig. Actually there was no comparison at all. He was a boy and Craig was a man, and that was all there was to it. He bore the same relationship to Craig that his silly hotrod bore to Craig's Mercedes.

"April," he said, "would you like to go for a ride?"

"Don't be ridiculous."

"Listen, we have to talk. You don't understand."

"I understand," she said sweetly. "You laid me yesterday and you can't get over it. Well, I can, Bill. I'm completely over it, and I'd just as soon not see you again. So hop in your car and—"

"April," he said. "Jesus, you don't understand. April, I don't think you're just another girl to lay and forget about. Maybe Danny felt that way but I'm not Danny. April, I want to talk to you and go places with you and spend time with you and get to know you. Do you know what I'm trying to say?"

"I don't really care."

His eyes blazed. "I'm trying to say that I'm in love with you, April."

She sighed. "That's interesting," she said. "Very interesting. Now get in your car and go away, Bill."

"Listen—"

"I listened. I'm not interested."

"Damn it, did I do something? If I did, tell me about it. I just don't get you, April."

"That's it exactly."

"Huh?"

"You just don't get me," she said. "Now go away, Bill. I'll see you around, if I can't help myself."

He ground the gears, raced the motor, and left a patch of

rubber on the street. She looked at it and laughed. Then she returned to the yard and stretched out in the sun.

CHAPTER 5

By five o'clock she had finished her shower. By five-ten she was dressed, and by a quarter after five she was nude again and pawing around for something better to wear. She rejected dress after dress, scurrying through her closet in a hectic rush to find the one garment which would suit the occasion better than any other.

A dress to be seduced by Craig in, she thought—a very special sort of dress. She remembered a line she had heard somewhere: "The ideal dress makes a man want to rip it off you," and she looked for that particular type of dress. The closest she came, ultimately, was a green affair which her mother had insisted made her look at least five years older. This, according to Mrs. North, was why the dress was unsuitable. It was also the main reason April had purchased it in the first place.

The top was silk, a tailored sort of top with a muted Chinese print. The skirt, tight and trim, was a darker cotton. Somehow the overall effect was the ultimate in sexiness but with no hint of cheapness. The skirt hugged her hips securely, swept in at her slender waist. The top was tight around her breasts, and the neckline dipped slightly to give a hint of the majestic cleavage below. Without being too obvious, the green dress managed to make quite clear the undeniable fact that April North had a highly desirable body.

She had bought it but she had never worn it. Antrim lacked occasions where such a dress would be suitable. She might have worn it to the senior prom, in fact had planned to do so. That was out now.

But she could wear it for Craig.

She had the dress halfway on when she stopped suddenly and peeled it off again. She remembered how Danny Duncan had struggled with the clasp on her bra, how he had worked her panties down over her hips. She didn't want Craig to struggle—although it was a good bet that his hands would be deft at such a task. She wanted it easy for him. She wanted to take off her dress and be nude beneath it. Completely, entirely nude. And ready for him.

When she put the green dress on again, there was nothing under it but April North. The silk blouse of it was sensuously luxurious against the tips of her big breasts, and her inner thighs rubbed together when she walked, rubbed in an earthy rhythm.

She studied herself in the mirror. I am sexy, she told herself. I am terribly sexy, and under this dress there is nothing but sexy little me—nothing but naked flesh.

Naked flesh.

She stayed in front of the mirror, combing and brushing her long hair. No pony tail tonight, she knew. No bun, no bangs, nothing but light brown hair falling freely over her shoulders. She put on a pair of plain black suede, high-heeled pumps. No stockings, she thought. No stockings, because she was not wearing a garter belt to hold them up. Just a body, a dress, and shoes.

She looked at her watch. He was coming for her at six and it was ten minutes before six already. Ordinarily she would have waited upstairs, then would have called to her mother that she would be down in a minute after he arrived. Then she would keep him waiting five minutes, maybe ten.

But she knew intuitively that this would not work with Craig. That particular sort of feminine deception would not impress him in the least. She left her room, walked downstairs, and took a seat in the living room.

Her mother appeared, the inevitable dishtowel in one hand. "A shame you'll miss dinner again," she said. "Two nights in a row. And you know how you love fried chicken."

"Craig's taking me to dinner."

"I know, April. Boys don't usually take you to dinner, do they?"

"Craig's older," she said. "Besides, his parents aren't living. If he didn't take me out, he'd have to eat alone."

"You could ask him to have supper with us, April. There's plenty of the chicken—"

She had to struggle to keep back laughter at the picture of Craig at a family dinner. She imagined all of them sitting around the table stuffing their mouths with fried chicken, wiping greasy hands on cotton napkins and talking about business at the drugstore, the latest item of importance before the Ladies' Aid, and Link's prowess at football. That would be just the way to start off an evening with Craig, she thought. That would send him screaming out of the house, leap into his Mercedes and point it for New York.

"Not tonight," she said gently.

"Not if you've made plans, I suppose. Some other night, April. Invite the poor boy over."

"Oh, I will."

"Not having any family—"

Something started to burn on the stove, and Mrs. North vanished hurriedly. April sighed. There was a cigarette in her purse and she wanted it desperately. But she could imagine her mother all upset at the idea of her smoking in front of a man. She sighed again, and the doorbell rang.

She answered the door herself. He smiled, then looked her over. His eyes started with her face and moved downward to her shoes, lingering with interest at certain areas. Then he gazed into her eyes again.

"Lovely," he said.

She took a breath. He was dressed exquisitely in a brass-buttoned summer-weight blazer and a pair of tailored Italian slacks. His hair was combed back and his moustache was neatly trimmed. His eyes, bright as beads, gleamed at her.

"Would you like to come in?"

"And meet the folks?" The sarcasm in his voice was almost gentle. "Of course, April. I'd love to."

They were in the car, racing along 68, and the wind was tossing her hair all over hell and gone. She let the wind flick ashes from her cigarette. Craig had impressed hell out of her parents, she thought. In just a few moments he had won them over forever. Her father now thought Craig was mature and level-headed, a young man astutely aware of the dangers of creeping socialism and the need to keep the government out of business. Her mother was just as certain that Craig regarded church and family in sacred awe, that he helped old ladies across streets and befriended stray cats.

Even Link had been impressed. In his eyes, Craig was strong and solid, a top athlete and a devil with the women. Which, she thought, was true enough.

"Where are we going, Craig?"

"Springfield."

"Springfield?"

"For dinner," he said. "Springfield is an ugly little town with very little to recommend it. It has to its name one good hotel, three fourth-rate whorehouses and one fine restaurant. One exceptionally fine restaurant, unbelievable for Ohio."

"What's the name of it?"

"Kardaman's," he said. "You'll like it."

She liked it. Kardaman's was located on a side street just a few doors off the main stem of the city. It was housed in a white frame dwelling set back a good distance from the street. A neatly painted signboard announced the restaurant's name and nothing more. A white-coated Negro greeted Craig by name and ushered them to a table. It was the only table in one small room off the main dining room. Through the window April could see the outskirts of Springfield. The Negro, whom Craig had addressed as Paul, lighted two candles with a wooden match, shook out the match, and hurried away.

"This is lovely," she said.

"I'm glad you like it."

"What's good here?"

"Drinks, first of all." A waiter came over and Craig ordered scotch on the rocks for both of them. When the drinks arrived they touched glasses and sipped the liquor. She was developing a taste for scotch, she thought. Soon she would know how to tell one brand from the next.

"Your parents are nice people," he said.

"I suppose so."

"They are, April. They're small-town to the core and there's a great deal that they do not and never will understand."

"Like me."

"Like you." He smiled. "Like anything outside their own specific frames of reference. Your father worries about pinkos in Washington and whether he'll sell enough condoms to pay the rent. Your mother worries about church affairs and reputations and hopes you'll marry a nice sweet boy who comes from a good dull family. And your brother wants to be a football hero so all the girls will lift their skirts for him. They're square as hell, but they're still nice people."

He sighed, smiling still. "I'm long-winded tonight. Mind if I order for both of us? I think I know what you'll like."

He did. He ordered something called beef Stroganoff, which she had never had before and it was delicious. He ordered a good bottle of red wine along with the meal. Afterward he ordered brandied coffee, which somehow settled everything in her stomach and in her mind as well.

She sat sipping her coffee and relaxing in complete luxury.

"This is wonderful," she said.

"The coffee?"

"The everything."

"You're happy, April?"

"Very happy."

"Let's get out of here," he said. "I want to make you even happier, April."

The Mercedes shifted down to second and the gears acted as a brake. The car slowed. Craig hit the brake and the sleek sports car glided to a perfect stop.

"We're home, April."

Her head was lighter than air. I feel pretty, she thought. I feel pretty and witty and bright. She stepped out of the car, looked once more at Craig's home. At dusk the house rose even more dramatically from the landscape. He took her arm and she leaned a little against him. They walked together to the door.

Without a word she followed him inside, standing patiently beside him while he closed and bolted the door. He turned, and all at once she was in his arms, her breasts drawn tight against his chest, her eyes closed, her heart beating against her ribs like an animal shaking its cage. His arms went around her. With one hand he stroked her silky hair; with the other he rubbed the small of her back until she tingled.

He kissed her. At first—but only for a moment—her lips and his merely brushed. Then her mouth opened and his tongue darted inside, a living flame that seared the roof of her mouth and seemed to set her own tongue on fire. She moaned softly, pressing still closer, and her lips and teeth closed around his tongue, imprisoned it, sucked on it and refused to let it escape.

The kiss lasted a long time.

When he released her she nearly fell to the floor. She was limp as the dishrag her mother always carried, limp and lifeless. And at the same time she was a woman on fire, a woman with the beginnings of a desperate craving burning in her.

"Craig—"

"Don't talk," he said.

He took her arm and led her across a room, down a hall, through a doorway. She looked around. They were in a bedroom and no room that she had ever seen was so completely bed-oriented. There was one bed the size of three beds, one huge brass bed that dominated a room which was large in its own right. He flicked a switch—evidently the whole house was wired for sound—and music came over the hidden speakers.

Not jazz—not this time. Not music like anything she had heard before. This was weird music, weird and wild and wonderful music.

Bedroom music.

He touched another switch. The overhead light went out, and a soft pale green glow from the walls illuminated the room. He turned once more to her, reached for her, and she went to him. And again he burned her mouth with a kiss.

The green dress buttoned in front. The silk top part had buttons, that is, and the top one was between the tops of her breasts. He opened the button and the blouse burst apart a bit. She felt the cool air on her breasts and drew in her breath sharply, excited by the sensation—excited, too, by his eyes on her breasts.

He opened each button in turn. The blouse fell all the way open and her breasts were exposed. He looked at them, admiration shining in his eyes, and his fingers reached out carelessly to brush the cherry tip of each soft white mound. Instantly her nipples reacted, stiffening and jutting forward. She was so excited she could barely breathe.

He cupped her breasts in his hands now. His thumbs and fingers manipulated the globes of flesh and she shivered all over.

Then he pushed her dress all the way down.

"Naked," he whispered. "Naked for me, April."

She could not speak.

"Naked and beautiful, April."

He kneeled before her and his hands went all over her body. Then he stood up, shrugged off his jacket, whipped off his tie, tore off his shirt. He had hair on his chest, she saw. And she threw her arms around him so that she could feel his hairy chest against her soft, tender breasts.

He released her again. She stood before him, trembling, and watched him remove the rest of his clothing. When he was nude she studied him, looked from his face to his feet. Her eyes locked again with his. Then, slowly, he moved closer. His arms encircled her body, lifted. He carried her to the bed and set her down gently upon a pale blue bedsheet.

He joined her there.

His hands were everywhere, touching, caressing, exciting. Her breasts tingled with the ecstasy of his touch. His mouth kissed hers, and then his lips left hers to plant a trail of hungry kisses down her throat to her breasts.

When he kissed her breasts something snapped inside her. She turned in to a hurricane, a cyclone, a whirlwind. Her hips churned spasmodically and her pulse soared. An aching need grew in her groin and spread throughout her entire body until she was aware of nothing but her need for him, of nothing but a tremendous aching void that needed to be filled.

His lips.

His hands.

Everywhere. Normal sensations withered away. The sensual music still played but she did not hear it. She saw nothing, smelled nothing, tasted nothing. She could only feel, and the intensity of her feeling was unbelievable. He touched her and she vibrated like a taut wire. He stroked her and she arched her back like a bow, ready for him, needing him too much to wait any longer.

"Now," he said.

And it began.

His mouth was glued to her mouth, his chest pressed against her breasts. Her winding legs pinned him to her, and their bodies moved together in a rhythm that was as old as humanity. She hugged him close, her arms around him, her nails digging involuntarily into his back.

Time stopped. Space spread out flatter than the desert and wider than the world. Everything was perfect now, absolutely perfect, and everything was getting better, steadily better, incredibly better, impossibly more perfect. She felt all the forces of her body crouching together, readying themselves for the spring, and she felt the world racing by her, and she felt her body and his body and nothing more.

Then passion broke for both of them at once. They reached the top of the mountain just as someone moved the mountain away, and they fell together belly-to-belly to the very bottom of the universe.

•   •   •

He had lighted a cigarette. He drew on it, inhaled smoke, and passed the cigarette to her. She took a drag. No cigarette had ever tasted so good. She gave it back to him and leaned back on her pillow. Her eyes closed and she took a slow breath.

She said, "I'm a woman now."

"Yes."

"I wasn't before, Craig. I was just a girl."

"You were ready to become a woman."

"I know. The other boys—they weren't anything. They never happened. Nothing before was ever anything like this. I didn't know anything could be like this."

He did not answer immediately. She opened her eyes and saw that he was smiling. He gave the cigarette to her once again and she took a drag. Her entire body was limp, every muscle entirely relaxed. She had never been so thoroughly exhausted in her life. Not tired—she had no desire to sleep. Simply exhausted, drained and used up and, strangely, fulfilled.

She reached over and touched him. "Such a wonderful thing," she said. "Little things mean a lot, I guess."

"Little?"

"Well—"

"If you keep doing that, you might note an increase in size, girl."

"Woman," she said, correcting him. "Was I good, Craig?"

"You were good."

She sighed, stretched, yawned. "I want to be good," she told him. "I want to be the best in the world."

"It's a noble ambition."

"Am I the best, Craig? The best you ever had?"

"No."

The answer surprised her. She raised herself up on one elbow and stared at him. "You could have said so," she said. "Even if you didn't mean it."

"I don't lie."

"Well, what was wrong with me?"

"Nothing was wrong with you, April."

"Then—"

"Relax," he told her. "My God, what sort of vanity could lead you to suspect that you could be the best woman I've ever had? You're practically devoid of experience. You've got a great deal of natural talent, but there's more to lovemaking than enthusiasm and a passionate nature. It's an art, April. Do you know who was the best woman I ever had?"

"Who?"

"A forty-five-year-old prostitute in Marseilles. She had most of her teeth missing and her stomach was lined with stretch marks because she'd given birth to three children in her lifetime. Some drunken sailor broke her nose once and the bones didn't heal properly, so her nose was bent. Her face would have stopped most clocks. But she knew more about sex than all the rest of the female world put together. Do you think you could compete with her?"

"I'd like to try."

He laughed. "Wonderful," he said. "You're delightful, April."

"Was I any good at all?"

"Do you care?"

"Yes," she said. "It's very important for me to be good for you."

"You were excellent. I never expected you to be as good as you were."

"I want to be better."

"You will be."

"I suppose I have a lot to learn, don't I?"

"Of course."

She drew a breath. "Will you teach me, Craig?"

"I'll teach you." He turned to her, and his hand found her breast. With the tip of his finger he drew a miniscule circle around her nipple.

"It's time for a lesson, April."

She took a deep breath and let it out slowly.

"I'm ready," she said.

Craig reminded her to take a shower before she went home. She relaxed under the spray of water, scrubbed herself thoroughly, rinsed the soap away. She dried herself off and dressed again. The perspiration was gone now, and the tell-tale odors of sex were dispelled. She put on fresh lipstick and studied her reflection in the mirror. There were still dark circles under her eyes, the stigmata of incandescent orgasm, but other than that she looked none the worse for wear. It didn't show, she thought. She would have looked just about the same after an inspired evening of hand-holding in a movie theater balcony. It didn't show.

Craig was waiting for her in the living room. She asked him how she looked. He told her she looked good enough to eat.

"Not now," she said. "You'd better take me home."

He laughed. The car was at the curb. She settled her behind in the bucket seat and he started the motor. The Mercedes came to life and headed down the dirt road like a greyhound after a mechanical rabbit.

"A nice night," he said.

"The best in my life."

"I was referring to the weather."

"Oh," she said. The air was cool, she noticed, and the stars were bright in the black sky. There was a refreshing breeze blowing and the speed of the sports car increased the flow of fresh air. She filled her lungs with the air, watched tree limbs sway gently in the breeze. It was autumn, and the trees were losing leaves. Yes, she decided, it was a beautiful night. A glorious night.

"You're right," she told him. "It's a beautiful night."

'You're a beautiful girl."

"Do you really think so?"

"Of course. I told you I don't lie, April."

"What do you like most about me?"

He told her.

"Oh," she said. "I mean next to that. I'm not counting that."

"Why not? It's the best part of you, April."

She giggled. "But you're the only person who knows about it. What do you like next best?"

"Your hands."

She had been expecting him to say that he liked her breasts next. His answer was a surprise. She looked at her hands. As far as she could see, they were just hands.

"My hands?"

"They're neat and dainty and very pretty."

A boy like Bill Piersall would never have noticed her hands. He would have noticed only those parts of her body intimately connected with sex. Craig was different, she thought. Vastly different.

"Thank you," she said.

"Don't thank me. You were fishing for a compliment, weren't you?"

"I suppose so."

"A compliment for these." He let go of the steering wheel with his right hand and tapped each breast in turn. "These were what you had in mind, weren't they?"

She giggled.

"Well, they pass muster, little girl. In case you didn't know already."

Craig pulled the car to a stop in front of her house. He told her it was only midnight and she could not believe him at first. She felt as though she had spent at least ten hours in bed with him. He opened the door for her and walked her to her front door. She took a key from her purse and fitted it in the lock.

"I'll see you soon," he said.

He did not kiss her. She smiled and he turned and walked back to his car. She pushed the door open, stepped inside, and closed the door after herself.

Her mother was knitting in the living room.

"You're home early," she said.

"Not so early."

"Well, early enough. Sometimes older boys don't respect a

young girl's curfew. They don't understand, being accustomed to keeping late hours themselves. But this Craig seems like a very thoughtful young man, April."

"He is, Mom."

"Your father likes him," Mrs. North went on. "Says he has a good head riding on his shoulders. And I must say he gave me the same impression, April."

She kept her smile back. So her father liked Craig.

God, maybe he'd offer him a job in the drugstore. That would be just the place for Craig Jeffers. She could see him now, filling prescriptions carefully and methodically. Well, she thought, there was something else he had filled, and he had done a magnificent job of it.

"Did he buy you dinner, April?"

"Yes, Mom."

"Where?"

"The Coachman," she said, naming a popular middle-class restaurant in Xenia. If she told her mother about Kardaman's, Mom would never believe her.

"That's a fine place, April. Did you enjoy your dinner?"

"Yes, Mom. It was nice."

"Well, it's a nice place. I hope it didn't cost him too much money?"

"Not too much." She smiled inwardly. Craig had placed two twenties and a ten on the table to cover the bill plus the tip. But there was no point in telling her mother about that.

"Although he seems to have quite a bit of money. That car he drives must have cost a pretty penny."

"Well, his parents left him some money."

"Of course," Mrs. North said. "Well, money never hurt a good man. Your father used to say that it was as easy to fall in love with a rich girl as a poor one. Of course, he married a poor one in the end. But just the same—"

"Yes, Mom."

It was getting good, she thought. Now the old lady was hearing wedding bells in the distance. She could hardly wait to tell Craig.

"April? You didn't kiss him goodnight, did you?"

"Why? Did you watch, Mom?"

The woman blushed. "Of course not," she said crisply. "I wouldn't spy on you, April."

"I didn't mean—"

"I just noticed that your lipstick wasn't smeared. My, you used to come home from dates with other boys with your lipstick smeared all over your face."

"Oh, I see."

"But you didn't kiss Craig?"

"No, Mom."

"Did he try to kiss you?"

It was very hard to keep from laughing. The whole idea of a long discussion about a goodnight kiss with a man who had just taken her to bed for several hours was ridiculous in the extreme. But she managed to keep a straight face.

"Not on the first date," she said.

"My," her mother said. "Your Craig really is a gentleman, isn't he?"

"Yes, Mom. He is. I'm pretty tired, Mom."

"Well, you just run along to bed, April."

She started for the stairs. She was tired—that was true enough. And she did want to get to bed. But more than anything else she wanted to end what was becoming the conversation of a lifetime with her mother. If this bit went on much longer she was simply going to crack up laughing and that was all there was to it.

"April—"

She sighed. "Yes, Mom?"

"I was concerned about your going out with an older man, you know."

"I thought so, Mom."

"I'm not concerned now. Older men are more settled, April. They don't feel compelled to prove themselves. I think you're probably—well, safer with an older man, April."

This time, as she ran headlong up the stairs, she laughed hysterically. It was just too much, just too funny.

CHAPTER 6

April focused her eyes upon the small leather-bound hymnal and sang the words to the song in a small clear voice. She did not really have to study the words, since the congregation sang "God Bless America" each Sunday in an effort to prove that a theory holding Protestant churches to be a hotbed of communism was markedly untrue as far as Antrim, Ohio was concerned. Still, by looking at the hymnal she could avoid looking elsewhere. Elsewhere took in a lot of ground. Elsewhere included the minister, and April North was young enough to have trouble looking steadily and soberly upon the steady and sober countenance of a minister of God just a few hours after a night of scintillating sin. That the minister would have approved of April's conduct was highly doubtful. And, although she hardly suspected that he could guess her conduct from the expression on her face, she preferred not to look at him.

Elsewhere also included Bill Piersall a few pews forward, Danny Duncan a little to her left, and Jim Bregger across the aisle on her right. She seemed to be surrounded by boys who either had gotten into her or who had tried. Bill, for one, qualified on both counts—he had taken his pleasure with her in the woods and he was ready for more.

She did not want to look at them.

G-o-d bless A-m-e-r-i-c-a—
Our home, s-w-e-e-t ho-o-o-ome.

God bless everything, she thought. She closed her hymnal and returned it to the rack where it belonged. She turned to kiss her mother and her father in turn, then followed them all out of the church. Sunday, she thought, should be abolished. What a God-awful way to spend a morning.

She had never objected to church before. Previously she had even looked forward to it. It was uplifting, in a way, and after a morning spent sitting primly in a clean dress between her parents in the small church she had generally felt a great deal better. But the time she had spent with Craig had changed her feelings on the subject. Craig was almost violently anti-religious, and after being with him she felt the same way.

She remembered an incident from the night before at his house. They were in bed together at the conclusion of their second bout of lovemaking—her "lesson"—and he looked at her suddenly and said, "You can go to hell now."

She didn't get it at first. She stared at him, thinking that he was telling her to get out and never darken his doorway again, and she wondered what she had done wrong. But he explained soon enough.

"You can go to hell," he repeated. "You've committed a cardinal sin and you can burn eternally as punishment for it. Do you know what you've done?"

"What?"

"You've slept with a man without being married to him. You've parted your lily-white thighs without benefit of clergy. This makes you a sinner, April dear."

"I don't feel like a sinner."

"You don't look like a sinner. Even with your pretty nipples pointing at the ceiling, you somehow don't resemble the popular stereotype of the sinner. Do you feel sinful, April?"

"Not just now," she joked. "Give me a minute to catch my breath, Craig."

"Do you know what the only sin is?"

"What?"

"Self-denial," he said solemnly. "That's the only sin in the world."

She closed her eyes briefly. Craig was right, she thought. He was living a good life, a life better by far than that of the sanctimonious hypocrites who cluttered up the world. You only live once, and the value of your life could be measured by the amount of pleasure you received in the course of that one lifetime of yours.

Suppose I had stayed a virgin, she thought. And suppose I was walking along the road and a car hit me. And killed me. And suppose I died a virgin. She opened her eyes. Bill Piersall was standing in front of her, a determined look in his eyes, his hands planted firmly on his hips. He was wearing a dark blue suit. It was the only suit he owned, and he wore it once a week, to church and once or twice a year to a formal dance—these were the only times he wore a suit.

"I have to talk to you, April."

She wondered how many suits Craig owned. At least a dozen, she decided. And a dozen sports jackets and a dozen pairs of shoes, and he probably paid as much for his underwear as William Piersall paid for his whole precious blue suit.

"You can't keep on giving me the cold shoulder like this, April. It's not right."

"What's wrong with it?"

"April—"

"You don't seem to understand," she said haughtily. "I do not like you. I do not care for your company. You bore me and annoy me."

He drew a breath. "I know what it is," he said.

"Do you?"

"I was reading," he said. "In a book."

"I didn't know you could read."

He went on doggedly while she wished he would simply give up and go away. But he would not. "I read about it," he said. "About what happens with a girl like you. You see, you're a good girl. Deep inside you're a good girl."

"I'm glad you think so."

"And you're not cheap," he pushed on. "So what you and I did, it made you feel all guilty. You get it? And you make up for this feeling guilty by taking it out on me. You don't want to blame yourself, so you blame me."

"You ought to be a psychiatrist."

He missed the sarcasm. "I read it," he said. "In a book."

"That's the best place to read things."

"They have stuff like it in newspapers, but the books are better. I could lend you the book if you want. You could read about it and know it better."

She yawned.

"What I want to tell you," he went on, "is I respect you."

"Thanks a lot."

"And I'm not just after you on account of sex or anything. I wouldn't even want to do it with you any more. I just want to be your friend."

She laughed now. She laughed in his face, imagining how Craig would roar when she told him about it. *I just want to be your friend.* It was too much.

"Can we be friends, April?"

"Distant friends."

"I'll keep my distance, April. I mean it. I just want us to go out on dates and things, and go for rides, and maybe have cokes together and talk—"

"Distant friends," she repeated. "Miles apart. In order to keep our relationship pure. I think we should see each other rarely. Otherwise our bodies will pull us together."

"Sure. I mean—"

"We'll see each other once a year," she said. "At Christmas time. We'll shake hands solemnly and go our separate ways. That way we won't run into danger of fleshly sins. That way our love will be a pure love, William."

He scratched his head. "You talk funny," he said.

"I talk English."

"Maybe. But not like everybody else."

"That's because I'm not like everybody else," she said. "And thank God for that."

"Look, April." He cleared his throat. "Listen—"

"Go to hell."

He stared at her.

"Drive there," she said, "in your silly rod. Have a flat tire in hell so you can't get back. Just leave me alone, Bill. I don't like you."

Her parents were a short distance away, hearing nothing but waiting for her to join them. She did and they headed homeward.

"Whom were you talking to?" her mother asked.

"Bill Piersall."

"A friend of yours?"

"He thinks so," she said. "I don't like him."

"He's a sharp guy," Link said. "You ever ride in that car of his?" She shook her head.

"It's great, April. You know, he built the whole thing himself. Set himself up with a tool shop in the garage and worked it all up. He bought the Model A for about fifty dollars, and he picked up a Chrysler engine, and hammered the body into shape and made a million changes to hop the car up, and it's a real bomb. Bill can outdrag anything else around."

She smiled softly. "What did you think of Craig's car?"

"The Benz?"

She nodded.

"Well," her brother said, "that's different."

"You like it?"

"It's the best car I ever saw," he said. His eyes were saucer-sized. "A 300-SL, for God's sake."

"Link—"

Link looked at his mother. "Sorry," he said. "For gosh sake, I mean. That's what I meant."

"That's better."

"But it's some car," he told April. "Craig a good driver?"

"The best."

"He'd have to be, with a car like that. Uh—you think I could ever get a ride with him?"

"Sure," she said.

"You mean it?"

"I mean it." In a whisper she added, "He might even let you drive."

"I can't get a license for a year."

"That's all right."

"You mean it, April?"

She nodded, smiling. They all loved Craig, she thought. They all were just about ready to worship at his feet.

And she loved him, too.

Monday morning meant school. Monday morning meant getting out of bed far too early, rubbing sleep out of her eyes, taking a fast shower and leaving the tub not quite awake, going down for breakfast and eating in a fog, drinking coffee, and plodding out of the door with a book under her arm.

Monday morning meant her home room, six rows of five desks each, a teacher in front and twenty-nine students around her. Kids who seemed years younger than herself, after being with Craig, after feeling like a mature woman.

Monday morning meant English first period, when she volunteered a comment on *Hamlet* that would never have occurred to her before she met Craig. She had always been a good student. But now she was more perceptive, able to think more deeply and to form her thoughts more coherently. Her teacher, a gray-haired, washed-out woman who had long ago given up any possible hope that any Antrim High student would someday say something intelligent, was patently amazed. And pleased.

"That's a very interesting comment, April," she said. "Did you come across the idea in your reading?"

"No, Miss Banner. It just came to me."

"You thought of it yourself?"

"That's right."

"Well, that's very fine, April."

Monday morning meant a study hall. The study hall was another classroom, five desks in a row, six rows of desks, with a spectacled teacher at the large desk in the front. In theory, at least, the study hall was a place for studying. This rarely happened. The study hall was a gossip arena, a place to make dates and spread news.

April was uncomfortable. She saw the way eyes followed her as she walked through the door and up an aisle to her desk. She heard buzzing, and she knew at once that they were buzzing about her. She wondered what they were saying. Telling each other she wasn't a virgin, she guessed. Telling that she was an easy make, and telling that she was dumb enough to brush off a big man like Bill Piersall, and wondering whom she was laying now.

Well, to hell with them. She did not care what they thought or what they said in whispers. They were children—she was a woman. Their words and thoughts did not concern her.

That was Monday morning. There were two more classes, a math ordeal and a Spanish class, but they were uninterestingly routine.

Monday morning gave way to Monday noon. April walked to her locker, opened it, took out her paper bag of lunch. She carried it up several flights of stairs to the school cafeteria on the top floor, went through the line to get a cup of black coffee and carried everything to a table near the window.

Before, she used to eat lunch with a group of girls. Her friends, she thought bitterly. She had never been close to any single one of them in particular. But they were her friends, the girls she talked to, the girls who talked to her.

They were not talking to her now.

Now she was a pariah, a non-virgin, a girl who had done IT and who seemed to like it. She was, in short, a girl with a reputation, and at Antrim High a reputation was something on the order of a venereal disease. A good girl—one without a reputation—could not chance a conversation with a bad girl—as though the reputation might be contagious, and could rub off on the good girl and make a bad girl out of her.

So April ate alone.

She did not mind. Actually, she thought, she was pleased to get away from that clutch of gabbing poultry. They were children, they were foolish and shallow and they belonged in a tiny and stupid town like Antrim. She had nothing to say to them and they had nothing to say to her, and she was glad to avoid them.

And the view from the window was preferable to the noise that she would be subjected to at the girls' table. This was much better, she told herself. She gnawed at a peanut-butter sandwich, sipped her coffee and relaxed.

But not all the girls ignored her. While she was finishing her coffee, she saw a diminutive blonde cross the cafeteria floor toward her table. The girl was Judy Liverpool and all at once April remembered how she had used Judy as an excuse that time when Craig had first picked her up. She wondered if her mother mentioned something to Mrs. Liverpool. That could mess things up, she thought. That could ruin everything, after she had managed to tie all the loose ends together so prettily.

"Hi, April." Judy was smiling shyly.

"Hi," April said. "Have a seat."

The little blonde hesitated only a moment. Then she sat down, looked at April, looked away, and finally looked at April again, her lips trembling.

"I wanted to talk to you," Judy said.

"Go ahead."

"I—people have been saying things, April."

"And you want to know if they're true?"

"No, that's not it at all."

April smiled. Judy was nervous and April was sorry she had snapped at her. Judy had always been a sweet kid, not at all bitchy as the other girls were inclined to be. Judy was serious and dreamy.

"What's the matter Judy?"

"I—oh, I don't know."

"You can tell me."

Judy's eyes were very wide now. "I want to know what it's like," she said. "That's all."

"What it's like?" April asked.

The words came in a rush. "Oh, God, April. They all say terrible things about you, make jokes and call you names and everything, but I think they're just jealous. You know so much now. You—you did it, you see, and we haven't, and I don't know about them, I mean I can only guess, but I know about me. And I want to know what it's like, April. To be a woman, to have a boy do it to you, to feel it, to—"

She covered Judy's small hand with her own. "Take it easy," she said soothingly. "Relax."

"Does it hurt?"

"A little. The first time."

"Does it—feel good?"

"There's nothing like it."

"Really good?"

"Perfect."

"Do you—how many times do you do *it*?"

"That depends."

"Sure. I mean—April?"

"Yes?"

"Doesn't it make you feel bad?"

"It makes me feel wonderful."

"Don't you think it's wrong?"

"No." She remembered what Craig had told her. "There's only one sin," she told Judy. "Self-denial."

Judy thought, nodded. "But your reputation," she said at once. "Don't you worry about it, April?"

"No."

"Don't you care what people think? What they say about you? How they look at you when you're walking down the street?"

"I don't care, Judy."

"Really?"

"Really. I just care about what I think is right."

As she watched Judy walk back to her table, April finished her coffee, set the cup down and smiled broadly. They talked about her, of course. They called her names and snickered behind her back.

But they also envied her.

She knew something they did not know, something they could not know until they had done what she had done. And they envied her this knowledge, envied her so deeply that one of them had needed to ask her what it was all about.

Let them talk about her, then. Because she was way ahead of them.

She was glad when school was over for the day. She went to her locker, put on her jacket, gathered up the books she would need that night. She tucked the books under one arm and walked out. It was a good day—fresh air, a crisp breeze, a clear sky. She filled her lungs with the smell of burning leaves, fresh autumn leaves raked and burned at the curbs, the particular smell of the season.

Bill Piersall was waiting for her.

"You don't seem to understand," she told him before he could utter a word. "I don't like you, I don't want to talk to you and you're just making things difficult for me. Why don't you get out of my life?"

"I want to give you a ride, April."

"I don't want one."

He managed to smile. It was hard for him and this pleased her. Evidently he was really pretty crushed—probably he had never had a girl give him the air quite so coolly before and it was a new experience for him. Well, fine. Let him crawl around on his hands and knees. She would push his face in the dirt and laugh like a hyena.

"You're going home now," he said. "Aren't you?"

"Probably."

"Well, why walk?"

"It's good exercise."

"Listen," he said. "I won't even talk to you if you don't want me to."

"That's a fine idea."

"I mean, in the car. I won't talk to you, I won't touch you, I won't do anything but drive you straight home. Don't you get it, April? I just want to be friends. I want to take you home—that's all. I swear it."

She sighed.

"How about it, April?"

His car was parked at the curb. She looked at the souped-up hot-rod and curled her lip in disdain. "I wouldn't ride in that bucket of bolts," she said. "Not even if I liked the driver."

"It's a good car, April."

"It's beautiful."

"It may not be much for looks," he said, "but it's what's under the hood that counts. I put plenty into that car, April. I did every bit of the work myself. I took the shell of an old Ford and made a car out of it, and you ought to feel how it runs. It's a peach."

"That's nice."

He forced another smile. "Just let me run you over to your house," he said. "Believe me, April, you'll never get a ride in a better car."

The timing could not have been more perfect. Just as he was saying this, hands on hips and smile on lips, April heard a roar, a most familiar roar, as a car took a corner two blocks away. She looked up and Bill looked up, and they saw Craig's Mercedes, sleek and lovely, burning up the street at a speed way over the legal limit. Craig dropped the car down into second, hit the brakes, and the Mercedes pulled up at the curb.

Bill was staring at it.

"Bill," she said, "I guess I'll never get a ride in a better car, will I?"

Then she told him what he could do with his camshaft. She wasn't too clear on what a camshaft was, but she guessed that one shaft was as good as the next for what she had in mind. She turned away from him, wanting to race to Craig, but controlling herself, playing the scene for all it was worth.

She walked like a queen to the Mercedes. Craig leaned across to open the door for her, and she stepped in regally, seating herself in the snug bucket seat, fastening the belt around her middle. She leaned over to kiss Craig quickly on the cheek, then turned around slightly just as Craig dropped the Mercedes into first and put the accelerator on the floor.

She would not have traded the expression on Bill's face for anything in the world.

Chapter 7

Together they laughed over Bill. Craig suggested that Bill had a great career ahead of him as a gas-pump jockey, April added that he might have trouble making change for a dollar and they laughed their heads off.

"Where are you taking me?" she asked suddenly.

"Home."

"My home?"

"God, no," he said. "I'd just as soon not make sad comments about the danger of the welfare state with your petit bourgeois father, if you don't mind."

"Dad's working."

"Or make church talk with your mother. Let's go to my place, April."

"Fine."

"You can cook me a dinner," he went on. "And then I'll help you with your homework. Or won't your mother let you out on a school night?"

"She likes to have me home. But since I'll be with you—"

"She'll know you're perfectly safe," he finished for her. "That's fine. You need a great deal of help with your homework, little girl."

She arched an eyebrow. "I thought I was doing fine."

"For a beginner."

"I still have a lot to learn?"

"Of course," he said. "It takes a lifetime to become an expert in the art of love."

The art of love, she thought. She liked the sound of the phrase. A woman who was good in bed was an artist, like a person who wrote or painted or acted. The notion seemed to make everything she did with Craig that much more proper and correct. It was not sin, not at all. It was art.

"I'll do my best," she said. "And maybe I can work my way up to a whorehouse in Marseilles."

"Maybe."

She glanced at him and he seemed quite serious. She shrugged and sighed. "It's nice weather," she said.

"Let's not talk about the weather."

"What should we talk about?"

"About dinner."

She bit her lip. "I don't cook very well," she said. "You'll have to put up with me."

"I'll try."

"What should I cook?"

"Whatever your best dish is."

She squeezed his hand. "I make a wicked peanut-butter sandwich," she said, "but it'll probably be pretty pallid after Kardaman's. Are you used to fancy cooking?"

"I'm used to good cooking. It doesn't have to be fancy."

"But it has to be good?"

"It's better that way," he said, grinning.

"Well," she said dubiously, "I'll see what I can do. But I'm not guaranteeing anything."

"You said the same thing about bed. And you did very well."

She closed her eyes. This was nice, she thought. Rocketing along in the Mercedes, heading for Craig's house where she would cook him a dinner just like—well, like a wife. This would be fun, a way to pretend, a way to have a good time.

She realized with a start that she wanted more than the pretense. She wanted to be Craig's wife. To be April Jeffers, Mrs. Craig Jeffers. She kept her eyes closed, afraid to let her expression give her away.

Because Craig would not approve.

Craig did not want a wife. He had not said this in so many words, but she knew it was so. He wanted a mistress and—since she functioned satisfactorily in that capacity—he was willing to spend time with her. But a man like Craig was by no means ripe for marriage. He cherished his independence far too much to throw it away easily.

Still, she was going to marry him.

To accomplish that, she knew, would take time. But in time he would love her, would love her so completely that he would want nothing more than to spend the rest of his life with her. She would have to play her cards close to her pretty chest to keep him from the realization that she had her cap set for him. But she would do what she had to do. She would give him her love until he returned it in full measure, and then he would ask her to marry him, and she would.

April Jeffers.

Mrs. Craig Jeffers.

• • •

She called her mother from Craig's house.

"This is April, Mom."

"Where are you, dear?"

"Craig picked me up after school," she said, honestly enough. "You know I've got a paper to write for English, on *Hamlet*."

"I know."

"Well, Craig majored in English at college. He took a great Shakespeare course and he's helping me with the paper. I'm over at his house now."

"At his house, April?"

"Well, sure."

"Why didn't you bring him here, April?"

"Well, he's got all his books here," she said. "And his notes. There's nothing wrong, is there, Mom?"

There was a pause. Then, "No, I don't suppose so, April. Just be careful, dear."

"Careful?"

Another pause. Then, "April, when you get home, I'd like to talk to you."

"What about?"

"I'll tell you when I see you. I heard something about your young man, April. I don't know that it's true, of course, but it's not too pleasant, and I'd like to discuss it with you."

"Mom—"

"Not now," her mother said. "Will you be home for dinner?"

"Well, we're eating here, and—"

"I see. I'll talk with you when you get home, April. And don't be too late. You have school tomorrow, you know."

"I know, Mom."

"Goodbye, April."

She heard the click as her mother replaced the receiver. For a moment she stood still, holding the dead phone in her hand. Then, slowly, she replaced it.

"Something wrong?"

"Nothing really," she told Craig. He had taken a quick shower while she phoned her mother and his body was still glistening with droplets of water. He had a towel wrapped around his waist.

"What's the matter with Mrs. North?"

"I don't know exactly. She said she wanted to talk to me."

"What about?"

"About you."

"Me?"

"Uh-huh. She said she heard something about you and she doesn't know if it's true, but she wants to talk about it. And she told me something else."

"What?"

"She told me to be careful."

He roared at that. "She means don't get pregnant," he said. "Wonderful."

"What do you suppose she heard?"

"That I play with girls," he said. "Did you know that, my dear?"

She grinned. "I wouldn't have believed it for the world."

"But it's true."

"Really?"

"Really"

"Now?"

"Now."

"Not with that towel on," she said. "I'll bet you can't do anything like that with that old towel on."

"Then do something about it."

She reached out. Her hands touched his chest, cool and moist from the shower. They found the towel, opened it and dropped it to the floor.

"My God," she said. "I have all these damn clothes on."

"Take them off."

"Should I?"

"You had better," he said. "Otherwise I'll tear 'em to shreds."

"It sounds like fun."

"But it might throw your mother, April."

She giggled. Then she pulled the sweater over her head. She was wearing a bra—if you went without one at school you bounced going up and down the stairs, and the boys had enough ideas about her as it was. She unhooked the bra and discarded it and her breasts leaped free.

"You like?"

"You're still overdressed, April."

She got the skirt off and kicked her shoes halfway across the room.

"You like?"

"You've still got your socks on," he said.

"I want to keep my socks on."

"You do?"

"You told me it's sexy when a girl wears stockings. What's wrong with socks?"

"Get them off, April."

Teasingly, she lifted one foot, peeled the sock down and off. Then she stood on that foot and removed the other sock. She threw both socks away, put her hands on her hips and posed.

"Look."

"Come here, April."

"No," she said playfully. "No, you have to catch me. Do you think you can catch me, Craig?"

He lunged for her, almost comical in his eagerness. He lunged and missed and she danced away, light on her feet, eyes flashing in excitement. She ducked behind a low-slung modern chair and he raced after her. This time, when he made his lunge, his hands brushed her breasts but she got free again, skipping into the center of the room, still, his touch had affected her. She was excited now, needing him, aching for him, but waiting for him to catch her and master her.

"Can't you catch me, Craig?"

He lunged and missed again.

"Damn you, April."

"Catch me, Craig."

And, of course, he did catch her. She tried to dodge behind the sofa but she was off-balance and caromed off the wall instead, and his arms snaked around her waist and dragged her to the floor. She thrilled with excitement that was half pleasure, half pain. His hands were everywhere, setting her afire, and her need grew.

He laughed. "Beg for it," he said. "Beg for it, April."

"Please—"

"Beg," he taunted her. "Tell me what you want."

She told him.

"Tell me what you want me to do to you."

She told him.

"Tell me how much you need it," he said. "Beg for it, burn for it, itch for it—tell me!"

She told him.

At last he rewarded her, burying himself in her soft hot body. Her flesh was pulsing now, flaming, and her hips were thrusting and her breasts were crushed beneath his hard chest. She locked him to her, making sure he wouldn't escape, making sure he would not retreat to leave her screaming in agony . . .

She cooked dinner, after a fashion. There was a huge barbecue pit in the backyard, and there were two prime sirloins in the refrigerator, and there were two old Idahoes in the potato bin, and with all that equipment any low-grade moron could have cooked dinner. Craig built a fire in the pit and she wrapped the potatoes in foil and tucked them away in the coals, then smeared the steaks with a little salt and a speck of pepper and chucked them onto the fire. The steaks came off the fire burned on the outside and raw in the middle, just as they should be, and the potatoes, improved with a tablespoon of sour cream and some chopped chives, were fine.

"You're a good cook," he told her.

"It was tricky."

"But good."

"How about dessert?"

"I know exactly what I want for dessert, little girl."

"Oh?"

"Don't smirk at me. Yes, I know what I want for dessert. I want you for dessert."

"It sounds like fun," she said. "But I'll go hungry. Did you ever think of that?"

"I thought of it."

"Well?"

He sighed mightily. "April," he said, "you have a lot to learn, little girl."

"I do?"

"Yes."

"Teach me, Craig."

He smiled gently. "You shall have dessert, too," he told her. "I could hardly bear to eat while another went hungry. Do you understand, April?"

And, some moments later, they were head-over-heels in love.

A few minutes past nine, she left the Mercedes and walked to her front door. The door was open. She went in and her mother and father were waiting for her in the living room. She kissed them both hello, hoping the brushing she had given her teeth was sufficiently thorough.

Her mother took her to one side. "I mentioned that I wanted to talk to you, April."

"Yes, Mom?"

"Let's go upstairs, dear. I don't want to upset your father, April."

They went upstairs, Mrs. North leading and April close behind her. Whatever Mom had heard about Craig, April thought, was undoubtedly true. Well, she would have to find a way to talk Mom out of what was bothering her. If her mother ordered her to stop seeing Craig there was going to be trouble. Because she would not dream of giving Craig up.

But the talk would not go that far, she thought. Maybe her mother was just going to give her the usual sex talk, and don't-let-boys-put-fingers-up-you routine, the save-it-for-your-husband bit. The old lady would probably fall over in a faint if she knew there was nothing left to save for a husband.

They went into April's room, closed the door. April sat on the edge of the bed while her mother took the one chair and planted her ample rump upon it.

"April—"

"Yes, Mom?"

Mrs. North sighed. "This may be difficult for both of us," she said. "Especially after the approval I've voiced over your Craig. But I've asked around about him, April, and—"

"Why, Mom?"

"Why, because you're dating him, dear. A mother wants to know the sort of young man her daughter is seeing."

"I see."

"And what I've heard is not—well, not exactly favorable. There are rumors about that boy, April."

There are probably more rumors about your own daughter, she wanted to say. How had her mother missed hearing about her? Everyone else in town seemed to know that April North was no longer a virgin. But her mother existed in a calm little dream world, untouched by truth.

She asked, "What kind of rumors?"

Mrs. North sighed again. "It's hard for me to tell you, April. He seems pleasant enough, but people in town have told me he's a mite wild. That he dates girls and seduces them—and he drives around in that car of his at very fast speeds and runs with a fast crowd. He drinks a great deal and—"

It was time for a counter-offensive.

"Mother," she said, "if you had told me this yesterday I wouldn't have believed you. But now I know what you mean. I understand."

"Did he—"

"Try anything? No, he didn't. Can I start at the beginning, Mom?"

"Why, of course."

She gathered her forces, her verbal soldiers. "I talked to Craig today," she said. "After I spoke to you. I mentioned what you said, how you wanted to talk to me about something you heard about Craig."

"I don't know that you should have told him, April."

"It was the right thing. Because he sat me down and he told me all about himself, Mom. It was quite a story."

"Oh?"

"He used to be very wild," she went on, inventing brilliantly, "when he was just a boy. Oh, you know how it is—his parents were rich and I guess they spoiled him something awful. He always had everything he wanted and he went to exclusive prep schools and he ran around with a wild crowd."

"That's what I heard."

"That was because he didn't have any responsibility," April went on. "He was rich and he didn't have to work and he was wild. But then his parents died. It was very sudden and all at once he was all alone."

"How dreadful!"

"I guess the shock made him settle down. All at once he was all alone in the world, with no one to love him or take care of him, and he saw that his past life was wrong and that he couldn't live that way any more."

"The poor boy."

She went on, elaborating on Craig's reformation, telling how he had joined the church again, and how he was serious and sincere, how he was a prince among men. As she talked, she watched the play of expressions across her mother's face. It was obvious that she was swallowing every last word.

Which, April thought, was fine. She felt pleased with herself. She was lying magnificently, playing to her mother skillfully, working every gambit in the book. Her mother's weak points were church and family, and these points played predominant roles in April's story.

"He told me he wouldn't have had anything to do with me before," she finished up. "Because he knows I'm a good girl from a good family, and that wasn't the sort of girl he was interested in before—before his parents died. He wanted wild girls then. Girls who would—well, you know."

"Of course, dear."

"But now he needs a girl he can respect. And he respects me, Mother."

Mrs. North beamed. "He well might," she said. "You're a girl deserving of respect."

"Well, I come from a good family. And I know the difference between right and wrong."

Mrs. North beamed more brightly. These were the key words, April thought. God, she should be an actress.

She finished and waited. Her mother sat silent for a moment or two, her head bobbing in thought. At last she raised her eyes.

"April," she said, "I'll tell you something, my dear. Quite often we tend to judge men and women differently, and this is as it ought to be. A man is different, April. A man is born with a certain amount of wanderlust in him, and a man often has to let loose and run free as the wind. A woman cannot do this. A woman must stay pure for the man she will someday marry."

"I know, Mother."

"But a man may sow wild oats, April. And I'd be the last to say that it's better for a man to hold himself in during his youth. Perhaps it's better for him to sow those wild oats then. The minister might not agree with me—"

"I know."

"—but you see what I mean. For if a man sows his wild oats in his young days, he can get these improper desires out of his system. He can settle down. He knows what is right and what is wrong, and he knows the taste of forbidden fruit is not all it's cracked up to be. So he learns to live life as it should be lived. Otherwise a man may run wild after marriage, and if that happens, may the Lord help his poor wife."

She felt like saying something about her own father, who had quite obviously never gotten around to sowing wild oats. But she stayed silent.

"Your Craig," her mother said. "Now there's a boy who ran

wild when he was young and who grew out of this wildness into something good and gentle and upstanding. A boy like that could make a good husband, April. A husband you'd never need to worry about."

Later, when her mother left the room, April laughed. She wondered if she would ever be able to talk to her mother again without laughing.

CHAPTER 8

Saturday night April North was dressing for a party.

Saturday night was sometimes party night. Antrim was fairly short on parties, but occasionally a clutch of high school students gathered at the home of a girl or boy, knocked off a case of beer, danced close, necked with lights out and stopped breathlessly short of anything really satisfying. These doings generally took place on Saturday night, with church facing the party-goers in the morning.

But April was not dressing for a high school party.

She was going to a much more exciting party, a party at Craig's house. She dressed again in the green silk-and-cotton affair she had worn on the night Craig took her to Kardaman's and made love to her in his big brass bed. At first she hadn't wanted to wear the same dress, but nothing else seemed appropriate.

"I don't have anything to wear," she had told Craig. And when he suggested the green dress, she voiced her objections.

"So what if I've seen you in it before?" he demanded. "I've seen you naked, and that doesn't bore me either. My friends haven't seen your dress. Wear it."

So she was wearing it. And again she was wearing nothing under it. Maybe I'm being sluttish, she thought. I could wear a bra, and I could wear a slip, and I could sure as hell wear a pair of panties.

But she did not want to.

She compromised by wearing stockings and a garter belt. Craig said it was exciting to make love to a girl wearing stockings. Well, he would get his chance. Sometime in the early morning all the guests would go home and she and Craig would be left alone with each other and—

He picked her up at eight. She kissed her mother and father good night and ran to the car where he was waiting for her. He opened the door and she got in.

"Let's go," he said. "It wouldn't do for us to be late. After all, I'm the host."

"Am I the hostess?"

"Sure."

"Good," she said.

The days since Monday had been good days. Her schoolwork had slipped a little, maybe, but she could keep her head above water in Antrim High without half-trying. And, while she had not been with Craig every day, she had enjoyed herself, had seen him every other day and had been truly alive while they were together. And now, for the first time she would be meeting his friends.

She wondered what they were like. As far as she could determine, Craig managed the difficult task of belonging to a group while remaining somehow aloof from it. He ran with a certain set of people, people like himself—young and sophisticated, moneyed and wild—yet at the same time he maintained a great degree of independence from the group. He preferred to spend a great deal of his time alone, away from people, and she had the feeling that he was secretly glad he could not be with her all the time. He valued his freedom, even treasured his time to himself, and she accepted him as he was.

But what would his friends be like? Even though he was independent, surely he would want his friends to approve of her. Suppose they did not? Suppose they thought she was just a hick from Antrim, a young and silly little girl who was not worth their time?

She wondered if his friends' reactions would alter Craig's opinion of her. If they disapproved of her, he might think less of her as a result. She did not want this to happen.

"Maybe your friends won't like me," she had said, a few days ago.

"They'll like you."

"How can you tell?"

"My friends always like a girl with breasts like these," he said. And then he had taken her breasts in his hands and the gesture had taken them out of the realm of serious discussion and into something else entirely.

Still, she worried. Outwardly calm, with one arm flung casually over the side of the car and a cigarette drooping from her lower lip, she was still quivering inwardly with the fear that Craig's friends would not care for her. While they might be duly impressed by her mammary development, this was not what she wanted. She had to be accepted wholly, not just as a body that could give a man pleasure.

"We're here," Craig said.

Inside the house, with the hi-fi on again, she helped him to get ready for the party. When her mother had a party—which, admittedly, was rare—preparations were complex. At least a dozen different sorts of salted nuts had to be set out, each variety in a different silver nut dish. Potato chips and cheese dip were comparably important. Occasionally her mother devoted several hours to the preparation of her cheese dips and she was known far and wide for them.

"But this gang is more interested in spirits than anything else," Craig said. "As long as the bar is well-stocked, the party's quite likely to turn out a success. A few extras, of course. A jar or two of pâté, some caviar and smoked oysters. That should do it."

"Do you have enough liquor?"

"Plenty," he told her. "Scotch, bourbon, rye, gin, vodka and cognac. Two bottles of each to start with, and reinforcements waiting in the cellar. There shouldn't be any shortages. Not even Ken Rutherford can exhaust our liquor reserves."

"Ken—"

"Rutherford," he said. "He has a hollow leg. His old man's a rich alcoholic who never hides the bottles after he passes out. Kenny-boy started lapping up the sauce at the ripe old age of twelve and he never did learn to quit. He has cirrhosis of the liver. Can you imagine that, April? The son of a bitch has cirrhosis at age twenty-three."

He paused, looked away vacantly. "He'll be dead in two years," he said, his tone matter-of-fact. "Or maybe tomorrow, as far as that goes."

"Shouldn't he stop drinking?"

"He'd just as soon die, April."

She turned away, fumbled for a cigarette. There were things Craig said to her occasionally that jarred her. This was one of them. How could a twenty-three-year-old boy accept death as a logical price to pay for drinking too much too often? The thought was terrifying. Was life that cheap?

Maybe it was. Maybe she was only showing her own lack of sophistication. But there was a thin line separating sophistication from insane dissipation and she was never quite sure where that line should be drawn.

"Will I have fun tonight, Craig?"

She saw him look at her, his eyes searching. "That's an odd question," he said. "Why did you ask that?"

"I don't know."

He put ice cubes in a pair of old-fashioned glasses and poured scotch over them. She sipped the whiskey, glad she had the drink now, knowing for the first time the meaning of definitely needing the stimulation. This was not as though she were an alcoholic, nothing like that. But she had had drinks before and she knew that they tended to relax her, to permit her to unwind. And she wanted to relax and unwind now.

She looked at Craig. The drink was not his first of the evening, and of course it would not be his last. He looked fairly drunk, she decided. His eyes were slightly glazed and his complexion was a little ruddier than usual.

He said, "You'll have fun, April."

"I hope so."

"You will. You'll be a bit lost at first, maybe, but after that you'll relax and enjoy it." He laughed. "When rape is inevitable, relax and enjoy it—an old saying from the Jeffers book of familiar quotations. You'll have a good time, April. You don't have to worry about it."

She nodded. "What will we do? At the party, I mean."

"Huh?"

"Well," she said, "we won't choose up sides and play charades. What will we do?"

He looked at her far a moment, then laughed. "Talk," he said. "Drink. Mingle. And eventually we may see some home movies. Does that sound like fun?"

"Home movies?"

"Just an attempt at humor," he said. "You'll see, April. We'll have a fine old time. Don't worry about it."

She finished her drink in a gulp, waiting for the alcohol to take hold and loosen her a little. Then she reached for the bottle and poured fresh scotch over the half-melted cubes of ice.

They were interesting people.

She had to grant that, right from the start. She was sitting on the low-slung couch with a man about thirty and a girl around the same age, perhaps a year to two older. The man had lost most of his hair in front and was compensating for the loss with a neatly trimmed black goatee. His name was Frank Evans and he was a reporter for the *Dayton Evening Star,* covering the police beat and doing general assignment work. He had sharp, inquisitive eyes and a high-pitched voice. He spoke quickly and did not seem to stop for breath.

The girl—or woman, really—wore dark glasses. Her dress was extreme, April thought. She wore leotards, black, and a tunic, green, and she used no lipstick and a great deal of eyeshadow. The tunic concealed most of her figure, but April could see that she had large, almost opulent breasts and long, strong legs. She was a little on the stocky side, with too much in the belly and more than too much in the rear, but while such imperfections might have kept her off the cover of *Vogue* they did not detract from her generally sexy appearance.

Her name was Margo Long. April was not sure exactly what she did. She seemed to be some sort of literary luminary, reviewing books for a Dayton paper and lecturing occasionally to women's groups. Right now she was busily engaged in the popular pastime of putting people down.

"These damned parties," she said. "I keep swearing not to go and every time another party comes up, there I am. I sit and watch Ken Rutherford put holes in his liver while Sue Maylor tries to make every male in the room and Larry Ellis sees how many girls he can shock. Look at them, will you?"

April looked. Ken Rutherford was easy to spot—he always had a glass in his hand and he was usually drinking from it. His eyes were vacant, his hair wild, his face pallid. April could not help being fascinated by him. He was quite thoroughly dissipated, a man on his way to an alcoholic grave, and he did not seem to give a damn.

Sue Maylor was on the other side of the room, talking to Craig and practically pushing her well-padded bosom into his face. She was a large girl with flaming red hair and a siren's body—Craig had told her once that Sue had laid almost every man she knew and that the few exceptions were homosexuals. Now the redhead was pressing against Craig, her hot little hands moving toward the front of his pants.

Get away from my man, April wanted to shout. But she knew enough to keep her mouth shut. Flirting was *de rigueur* at these parties, she realized, and fairly advanced petting went by the name of flirting. She would be eternally labeled gauche if she made her objections known.

"Hell of a way to spend an evening," Margo Long said. "I'd rather stay home with a good man and wear out a set of bedsprings. But here I am, damn it. I think I'll go find a drink."

She got up abruptly and headed across the room to the bar. April turned to Frank Evans. "If she doesn't like these parties—"

"Then why does she come here?" Frank smiled sadly. "Because there's no place else for her to go, I'd say. Don't let her fool you, April. She talks a good game but she doesn't hate the party as much as she makes out. It's a pose with her. She dislikes the party to a degree, and I suppose she loathes most of the people here. But she'd much rather come over to Craig's house than sit at home alone."

"I see."

He took a pipe and a pouch of tobacco from his jacket pocket and went through the laborious routine of cramming tobacco into the bowl and lighting it with a butane lighter. When the pipe was going properly he turned to her and smiled again, the same sad smile.

"Margo's an unhappy woman," he said. "You heard her line about wearing out bedsprings? She'd like nothing better, I suppose. But she's not a promiscuous gal and she has trouble holding onto a man for long. She can attract a guy, sure—but that's not all there is to it. Margo's the dominant type, has to run the show or she goes nuts. Not every man likes to be dominated— damn few of them do—and Margo wouldn't settle for the Casper

Milquetoast variety. She wants a strong man and no strong man will stick with her."

April said, "That's a shame."

"It's her personal tragedy. We all have a personal tragedy, April. Every last one of us."

"We do?"

"Of course. Otherwise we wouldn't be here." He drew on the pipe and blew out a cloud of smoke. "Mine is simple enough. I was born in Dayton. I hate Dayton. I always wanted to get out of this backwater and into the big time. And I never did."

"How come?"

He shrugged. "A perfect question. Unhappily, there's no perfect answer. I had big dreams, April. Correspondent for the *Times*, political columnist, best-selling novelist. Dreams are cheap, April. Remember the song in *Gypsy*? *'Some people sit on their butts, Got the dream but not the guts'*—that sums up Franklin Evans, Frank to his friends and enemies alike. Dayton pays me a hundred dollars a week. Dayton gives me steady work, so steady I'm scared to leave it. And I stay and remain bored and go to parties at Craig's house."

April found nothing to say. Frank let out a long sigh and followed it with a mirthless chuckle.

"So there's my tragedy. And it's not all that tragic. You need a heroic figure for real tragedy and I'm afraid I don't quite fit the bill. But how about you, April North? My God, you're far too young to be tragic. Why don't you go home?"

She stared at him. "I don't understand," she said.

"You should go home. You're getting yourself in for the wrong kind of scene here, April North."

"Why do you call me by my full name?"

"Because it's a remarkable name. You're just messing yourself up, hanging around with a crowd of has-beens and nymphomaniacs and alcoholics. Has-beens? Never-wases is more like it. Stick around here and you'll be just like everybody else. Are you living with Craig, April North?"

She flushed. "I live at home," she said. "With my parents."

"But you sleep with Craig?"

"That's none of your business."

"Probably not. It's your business, though."

"What do you mean?"

His pipe had gone out. She waited, trembling slightly, while he thumbed the butane lighter and sucked at the pipe stem, blowing smoke from the side of his mouth. When the pipe was lighted evenly he closed the lighter and dropped it into his pocket. He regarded the bowl of the pipe thoughtfully, drew on it a few more times, and then took it again from his mouth.

"I mean he'll ruin you," he said.

She said nothing.

"He'll make a mess of you, April North. He'll have you crawling on your hands and knees and when he shoves you away you'll be rotten inside. He's worked that way with more women than you've lived years, which isn't saying too much, I suspect. He turns decent girls into whores and takes their backbones away in the process. He's no good, April."

"He has what he wants," she said.

"He does?"

"He isn't working for five thousand a year in a job he hates," she said angrily. "He doesn't dream about a New York job he'll never have or a book he'll never write. He's far away in front of you, Mr. Evans."

The words hurt him. She saw his shoulders sag and felt sorry for what she had said but not sorry enough to apologize. He stood up slowly, turning to her.

"Some day you'll realize that Craig is a failure himself," he said. "And by then it will be too late. For you, I mean."

He left her to wonder what he meant.

Larry Ellis was short and stocky, with a sneer always present on his thin lips and a look of profound disenchantment never leaving his icy blue eyes. He had backed her into a corner and she held a cigarette ready before her, knowing that nothing could stop an aggressive male the way a lighted cigarette could. Yet he did not seem ready to make a pass at her.

"Don't go into the bedroom," he said. "Sue Maylor's in there. Know what she's doing, kid?"

"What?"

He laughed wickedly. He said, "I guess you are interested, aren't you? You know I could kind of go for you."

"I'm complimented."

She felt herself blushing. His hand reached out, calmly and dispassionately, and encircled her breast. He squeezed and her own reaction completely surprised her. She loathed Larry Ellis with a vengeance and would not go to bed with him for all the coffee in Brazil, but his hand on her breast was enough to set her off. She felt the nipple stiffen, seemingly of its own accord, and she felt familiar jolts of desire coursing through her firm young body. She hated Larry Ellis, hated him and wished he would leave her alone. But the fact remained that she was getting excited.

He said confidently, "How about it, April, kid? How do you want it?"

"You're disgusting. Let go of me."

He released her breast, then neatly flicked the nipple with his thumbnail. Her knees felt weak and she wanted to cry.

"I suppose you think that's funny?"

She finally got rid of him. He tried to shock, she knew, but he had merely disgusted her.

Something else gave her the shock.

She was on her way to the bathroom. She paused to light a cigarette, and a bedroom door, opened. Two people came through that door.

The girl was Sue Maynor. And April recognized the man.

Craig.

There was a long minute, a long, unhappy and uncomfortable minute while she simply stood staring at him, her mind making the necessary connections haltingly.

The picture sickened her.

Craig, her Craig, a participant in the action. Her man with that red-haired slut.

Craig was looking at April, saying something to her. But she could not hear a word. Her mind was doing cartwheels and she knew that any moment she would be sick to her stomach. Craig was saying something to her, and the red-headed whore was looking at her, smirking at her, and it was all too much.

April ran.

She scurried past them, and raced down the carpeted hallway and into the bathroom. The room was empty. She ducked into it, pulled the door shut, and twisted the key in the lock. She drew a deep breath, shuddered. Her stomach was doing handstands. She went over to the toilet, yanked up the seat, and spent several minutes throwing up.

When she had finished, she washed her hands and face with cold water and sat down, trying to think.

Craig.

That hurt her.

Her man, the man she loved, had made love to another girl. Her man, who meant everything to her, had cheated on her. And now what was she going to do?

She had no idea. She could leave, give up Craig forever as Frank Evans had advised her to do. But she did not want to leave, could not face going back to life as an average little student at Antrim High. Craig was too important, and his friends were too important—no, she could not do that.

What could she do?

She wasn't sure. She stood up finally, unlocked the door, went back to join the party. Fortunately not many people had seen her headlong flight, and those who had did not know what had prompted it.

Craig was at the bar.

"Hi," she said. "I could definitely use a drink."

He asked her what the matter was.

"Too much scotch," she said. "I guess I don't hold my liquor very well. At least I didn't ruin the hall carpet."

"You went by so fast—"

"I know," she said. "I was getting green around the gills. But I'm ready to start again."

He gave her a drink and she drained it.

CHAPTER 9

She was very drunk.

She sat on the couch, alone now, listening to the music that played on the hi-fi system and watching the proceedings. There were not too many proceedings left to watch. Most of the guests had managed to pair off into couples, or to make up otherwise acceptable groups, and had hence repaired to bedrooms for fun and frolic. Larry Ellis was off taking a shower with a girl; April had seen them stroll by, Larry's hand buried in the girl's blouse and his nasal voice explaining quite explicitly just where he was going to soap her, and just where she was going to soap him, and just what they were going to do standing up.

One couple was dancing now. The girl had removed dress and bra and the man had taken off his shirt. Both were barefoot and naked from the waist up. They swayed slowly together, their bodies tight in passion. Once they parted momentarily and April could see the girl's pink nipples. They were hard as little rocks.

Craig had been with her for awhile. Craig had taken her into a bedroom, and Craig had undressed her, and Craig had made love to her. That had been good in a way, and she had needed it. But somehow it had left her unsatisfied. She was still hot as a pistol, still needed something desperately. Craig was gone now and she did not know whom he was with or what they were doing. Nor did she give a damn.

God, she was drunk.

Not just high, with her head pleasantly light and her eyes pleasantly glazed. That stage had come and gone long ago. Now she was unable to stand without swaying, unable to walk without reeling. Her head was off in its own private world and her body was at once tired and hungry.

And they were having an orgy.

Not exactly an orgy, she thought. The Romans would have thought it pallid beyond description. And Craig had told her of orgy scenes he had been in which were far more shocking than what was going on at the Jeffers home. Yet it was still an orgy as far as she was concerned. Men were going off with girls, carting them to bedrooms, laying them and leaving them, taking fresh partners and starting in anew. If that wasn't an orgy, then what in the name of hell was it?

She turned slightly and her head ached. There was a girl sitting next to her.

"An orgy," April said.

"Really, honey? It's an idea, I suppose."

April tried to focus her vision. The girl, she saw, was Margo Long. Margo, who had waxed so vitriolic on the subject of Craig's parties and the people attending them. Margo was about half in the bag herself, she realized. But she carried her liquor better than April North. She looked cool and detached, calm and relaxed.

"Jus' a goddam orgy," April said. "All at once every thin' starts happenin.'"

"Is something the matter, honey?"

"I don't know. I need a drink."

She stayed where she was while Margo obediently crossed the room and poured liquor on ice. She returned, gave the glass to April.

"It was scotch, wasn't it?"

"It started that way. I tried vodka somewhere in the middle, but I'm back with scotch now."

"Then may the Lord help you in the morning. You need this drink like a hole in the head, honey."

"I guess so."

While she sipped the scotch, Margo looked at her quizzically. "Someone must have handed you a rough time," she said softly. "You want to talk about it?"

"Gotta talk to someone."

"You can talk to me, honey."

"Can I?" April pursed her lips. "Everybody talks. Chatter, chatter, chatter. Like magpies. Ever see a magpie?"

"Nope."

"Neither did I. Gotta talk to someone who listens. You wanna listen to me?"

"Sure, honey," Margo said. She reached out, patted April gently on the knee. Her hands were very soft, April noticed. Soft and cool and infinitely gentle.

"Come with me, April."

"Where?"

"Outside. There's a chaise in the garden. We can talk there without interruption."

"Okay."

"And the cool air will sober you up a little."

"Don't wanna sober," April said. "Wanna drunk."

"Come with me, honey."

She was standing now, with Margo supporting her, an arm around her waist. And she was walking, managing somehow to make one foot go before the other in a relatively orderly fashion. They walked through Craig's house, out the back door and into the garden. As they passed closed doors, she wondered just which door Craig was behind, and with whom. Not that she really cared, of course. Not that she gave a damn—

The fresh air jolted her. She filled her lungs and her head cleared a little. She was still drunk, of course, still stoned out of her ever-loving mind, but the fresh air did make a great difference. She didn't feel sick any more and her head worked a good deal better.

"Sit down with me, April."

The chaise where they sat was larger than the usual run of garden furniture, about the size of a double bed. A plastic affair with a pale yellow terrycloth cover, the chaise was springy and comfortable.

"Kick off your shoes, April. Relax a little."

She took her shoes off.

"You could take off your dress, too. Just sit around in bra and panties. The cool night air would feel wonderful on bare skin, April."

That sounded fine. But she remembered that sitting around in bra and panties might be difficult, since she had neither. She looked at Margo. The older woman was perfectly calm, perfectly lovely in the half-fight that filtered out to them from the noisy house. An opulent figure, April thought. Lush breasts and a lush belly and a lush behind. A big woman, and a lushly pretty one.

And I, she thought, am just a lush.

"Can't strip," she said. "Nothing under the dress."

"Left your underwear inside?"

"Nope. Left it home. Didn't wear any."

"Really?"

"Wanted to be sexy," she said. "For Craig, because I love Craig. But he laid another girl."

"He generally does," Margo said.

"That Sue Maynor."

"Oh, hell. Everybody lays Sue Maynor."

"Guess so. I didn't want him to. He can lay me and nobody else, the bastard."

"Poor April," Margo said. "Listen, honey, I've got an idea. Why not take off that dress, after all? Then you can stretch out on the couch here and I'll massage your back. It'll make you feel a hell of a lot better."

"But I'll be naked."

"So what? I'll strip down, too. Nobody is going to see us, April. They're all in the goddam house laying each other. And there's not a neighbor for five miles in any direction. Strip down, honey."

Somewhere in the back of her mind, a little voice was telling her to for God's sake not be a damned fool, because something fishy was going on. She chose not to hear the voice. Margo was a friend, a gentle and considerate friend. And Margo was going to rub her back, and it would make her feel wonderful.

What was wrong with that?

Nothing at all.

She got out of the dress. Margo had gotten out of her own leotards and tunic in the meantime, and was left with bra, half-slip, panties. Margo's figure looked even better now, April noticed. Margo looked feminine, warm, ample.

"Want to help me with the bra, April?"

She fumbled drunkenly with the clasp, finally got it open. Margo turned then, and she saw how perfect Margo's breasts were, how large and well shaped.

"See anything interesting, honey?"

April blushed.

"You really shouldn't have to stare at me," Margo went on. "Not the way you're built. God, I wish I were young again. Although I never shaped up that perfectly, not at any age. You look good, April. You really look wonderful."

She sat silently while Margo took off April's own undergarment. For a moment April was embarrassed. But then Margo told her to lie down on her stomach, and she stretched out and closed her eyes and the embarrassment vanished.

"Now just relax," Margo was saying. "Just relax, honey. This will feel fine."

Margo began to massage her back and April felt the tension draining from her body. Her eyes were closed and her muscles began to relax, to lose the feeling of insufferable tightness that had plagued her ever since she had seen Craig leaving the bedroom with Sue Maynor. She felt nothing but the terrycloth beneath her and Margo's hands on her, on her back, rubbing her neck, stroking, touching, helping her to feel better.

"Got to make you feel good," Margo said. "You're so beautiful, April. Do you have any idea how beautiful you are?"

Hands that did wonderful things to her naked flesh. Hands that rubbed her back, pressed the small of her back, came around the sides to massage her ribs. Gentle hands yet strong hands, almost masculine hands, yet so soft—

"Craig Jeffers is an ass," Margo said. "Any man who could pass up something like you for a slut like Maynor isn't worth the powder to blow him to hell. You've got a nice behind, honey. Did anyone ever tell you what a sweet little rump you've got?"

Hands that touched her buttocks now, patting and caressing, touching bare flesh. Hands that stroked her thighs, squeezing and patting the tired muscles and making her feel much better, much looser, much happier.

"So beautiful—"

She felt Margo's lips at the back of her neck, kissing her. Now why on earth would Margo want to kiss her? Yet it felt nice. Margo nibbled at the nape of her neck, spread a row of glowing kisses down the center of her back. She felt Margo lower herself upon her, felt the weight of the woman, felt two firm peaks of flesh that were Margo's breasts pressing against her back.

Margo's breasts were so warm.

Margo lay upon her, holding her, touching her, massaging her. And kissing her. And the whole world was light and airy, light and dreamy, light and lovely, and she was floating high in the sky on a terrycloth cloud.

"April."

She sighed softly, happily.

"Roll over, April."

"Why?"

"So I can do you in front."

The explanation was a fine one. She rolled over, her eyes still closed, and she heard the sudden and worshipful intake of breath as Margo saw the full beauty of her naked body. Margo's hands touched her now, holding her at the waist, massaging her flat stomach and stroking her hips.

Then, suddenly, Margo was holding her breasts.

The contact was electrifying. All at once the edge of the drunkenness was broken and all at once reality returned. She knew, now. She knew that this was not a massage, that it was not friendship, that it was in fact nothing more or less than lesbian love.

And she didn't care.

Margo's voice: "April, they're awful. Men are awful. They take a girl and they ruin her. They make a slave out of her. But I won't ruin you, honey. I'll be good to you, honey."

Margo kissed her. Margo's mouth was soft, incredibly soft, and kissing Margo was not at all like kissing a man. Her mouth opened to admit Margo's tongue, and then she felt Margo's good woman's body coming down on top of her own body, breasts against breasts, belly against belly, loins against loins. She put her arms around Margo, holding her close, and with her mouth she accepted the full intensity of Margo's kiss.

The world was swimming now. No, not swimming—floating, floating on its back with its eyes closed, floating in a blue-green sea of cool molten lead. April North was drunk. April North was naked as a jaybird in the great outdoors, with the air cool on her warm bare skin. April North was lying under a lesbian, was kissing and being kissed by a heavy-breasted sweet-mouthed woman. April North was enjoying all of this.

Margo's lips: leaving hers now, moving to kiss her cheek, to drop kisses on her tightly shut eyelids, to drink at her throat and move gently downward.

Margo's hands: on her breasts again, flexing the taut flesh, tugging hungrily at the firm nipples, cupping the mounds of female softness and teasing April into a desperate response.

Margo's mouth: Moving downward into the valley between those breasts, and now she could feel Margo's cheeks between her own breasts, soft and cool, and then she could feel Margo kissing her breasts, kissing the flesh, kissing the nipples, kissing and kissing and kissing with lips and tongue and

and

and

and

now the world was inverted, and Margo was inverted, over her, holding her. And now April was caught up in passion, alive with passion, thrilled by a passion unlike anything she had ever known before. Now the world was rocking in a motion older than Adam and Eve ...

Faster.

Faster.

Faster—

Then, at last, peace.

Dawn awoke her, sending shivers of light beating against her closed eyelids, and April opened her eyes to blink and shuddered violently. There was a moment during which she was quite uncertain where she was or how she had gotten there. Then memory came in a flash, and she recalled everything, and she sat up shaking.

She was still naked. She was still on the terry cloth-covered chaise in Craig's garden.

Margo was gone.

Well, she thought, thank God for that. Waking up alone under this particular set of circumstances was impossible enough. Margo's presence would have made the morning even harder to take.

She stood up, and then all the drinking and all the everything else caught up with her. Knees buckled. She fell to the grass and heaved. She lay there and retched uncontrollably for several minutes.

This time she was even weaker when she stood up, but the nausea had vanished at least for the time being. Outdoor nudity was far less romantic when you were sober and when the sun was shining. She fumbled around for her dress, got into it, and slipped her shoes on. The dress was slightly damp from the dew. She wished she had been a little less dramatic and a little less sexy and a little more practical. Bra and panties would have helped now, and she should have worn them in the first place.

She needed a cigarette.

The back door of Craig's house was open and she went inside, taking a cigarette from a crumpled pack in the living room. She found a match, lit it, and took a deep drag. The living room was a shambles with empty glasses, empty bottles and overflowing ash trays scattered throughout the large room. The smell of dissipation, compounded of alcohol and vomit and sex, pervaded the atmosphere.

A wall clock indicated quarter to seven. In the morning. And she had still not come home.

God, she thought.

What explanation would satisfy her mother? None, probably. She was up the well-known creek in a lead canoe, and she didn't even have a paddle. No lie she could possibly dream up would work this time. She had gone to a party after dinner Saturday night and she was coming home on Sunday morning, and that had a funny smell to it no matter how you embellished it.

Then she realized something, and she laughed. The full humor of it hit her and she rolled around on the floor, laughing like a lunatic, holding her sides to keep them from splitting.

This was Sunday morning.

She had to hurry home to go to church with the family.

She took a last drag on her cigarette and ground it out in a copper ash tray already overflowing. She found another cigarette in the crumpled pack and got it going. She sat down—because it was hard to stand up now, hard to keep on her feet—and she tried to make out just what had happened to her. Everything had happened to her.

Everything, starting with an evening of heavy drinking and sophisticated small talk. Then Craig playing orgy-master with that redheaded Maynor bitch. Then throwing up in the john, going to bed with Craig, getting drunk as a skunk and playing lesbian games with Margo Long on the chaise in the back yard. And waking up.

And now she was sitting alone in the living room and wanting only to go home, where she belonged. She ground out the second cigarette and walked through the house looking for Craig. She tried one room, and there were two sleeping bodies on the bed, but Craig was not one of them. Frank Evans was, and so was Sue

Maynor. She had to laugh—suave and polished Frank, the deep-talking pipe-smoker, was just as human as anyone else. He had taken his turn with Slutty Sue like every other man at the party.

She left the room quietly, closing the door. She tried another room, the bedroom where she and Craig had made love so many times. And this time she found him. He was lying on his back, mouth open, eyes closed. He was snoring, and all at once he did not look romantic or debonair at all. He looked like a bum, a drunken bum sleeping off a wine binge in a pig sty. For there was a pig with him.

A blonde pig with big breasts and smeared lipstick. April glanced from one to the other. I loved him, she thought. I actually loved the rotten son of a bitch. And she wondered what he and the blonde pig had done, and how many times, and—

She left the room.

She could not talk to Craig, obviously. Not now and not ever, as far as she was concerned. He was rotten and filthy and she would be damned a dozen times before she would try to wake him from his sleep with the blonde bitch to take her home.

But she could not walk, either. Home was too far away. So just what could she do, damn it?

Cars were parked in front. She went from one to the other and finally found a blue Pontiac with Dayton plates and keys in the ignition. She wondered who had been dumb enough to leave the keys, and silently thanked whoever it was for his or her stupidity. She climbed into the car, got behind the wheel, and sat.

She would have to go home. She did not expect a brass band at seven in the morning, but they would have to take her in and they would have to leave her alone. She could make up some sort of story—a car accident, trouble of one sort or another, anything that would placate them for a little while.

She turned the key in the ignition, stepped on the gas and started home. She knew the route. She had driven it often enough in Craig's Mercedes.

Craig—Craig Jeffers. She had loved him, she knew, and she did not love him any more. She could not understand it—he had always wanted her so much, had spent such a great deal of time with her, had seemed to love her so deeply. And yet he had been able to toss her over and go to bed with other girls. With Sue Maynor, and with the blonde tramp, and with God knew how many others.

Why?

Not because she was no good. She could not believe that. She knew that he had told her repeatedly how good she was, knew how wondrously exhausted she could make him. She remembered how he had cried out one time at the crucial instant, his nails digging into her shoulder, his face contorted in a mixed expression of pleasure and pain. There was nothing Sue Maynor could give him that she could not give him as well or better.

Why, then?

She sighed. She needed a cigarette but there was none around. She kept her mind on her driving, heading toward town and home.

They did not believe her.

When she went through the door her mother was standing with her hands on her hips and a fierce expression on her face.

Her father's face was drawn with worry and anger in more or less equal proportions.

This will have to be good, she thought.

"All right," her mother said. "Start talking, April."

She made up her story as she went along, an unlikely story about Craig having a malaria attack and how she had to nurse him through the night and pile him up with blankets and put hot compresses on his feverish head.

"He caught it in Italy," she explained. "He was there one winter and he caught malaria and he still gets attacks now and then. They say you never get over it. You can be cured and still get terrible attacks years later."

"And you couldn't even call, April?"

"Well, Mom—"

"We were up all night waiting for you," her father cut in. "You could have called us, April."

"Well, Dad—"

"April," her mother said, "I don't believe you."

"What?"

"I said I don't believe you. This story about malaria. I think you've been telling us stories all along. Why, I met Judy Liverpool's mother the other day and mentioned how nice it was of her to have you over for dinner and she said you hadn't been there at all. Where were you that night, April?"

"At Judy's," she said desperately. "Look, maybe Judy's mother forgot. I mean, it was over a week ago, and—"

"April." Her mother stopped, then sighed. "I don't want to discuss it now. Not today, not on the Lord's day. Are you coming to church with us, April?"

If you lie, she thought, you have to stick to it "I can't," she said angrily. "I was up all night and didn't so much as close my eyes. The fever broke finally but it was horrible. Around three in the morning Craig was having horrible hallucinations and everything. I never saw anything like it. Now I'm exhausted. I think I'll go to bed for awhile, if you don't mind."

They said they did not mind, but obviously they did mind. They did not believe her. Once their belief was shattered in one respect, they would question every single thing she told them from then on.

This was going to be bad.

They trooped off to church. April took a succession of hot baths and ate a full breakfast. When they came home she was sleeping soundly, and they let her sleep until dinner time. Dinner was an ordeal, with a good deal of cross-questioning and a generally unhappy atmosphere. The only thing to do, she decided, was to brazen it out.

"I'd better get back to him," she said after dinner. "I'll have to take the Pontiac. If he feels okay he can drive me back."

Her father offered to run her over but she managed to brush the offer aside. She left the house, dressed comfortably now in jeans and a sweater, and drove the Pontiac to Craig's home.

Chapter 10

The Pontiac was big and bulky. Cars, she thought, taking the turn off onto the narrow road that led to Craig's house. You could tell the whole story in terms of cars. A green Oldsmobile a year old, where Dan Duncan had claimed her virginity in the back seat on a Saturday night. When was that? Two weeks ago. Just two weeks ago.

And the Mercedes-Benz, the sleek 300-SL that had stopped for her when she had been on her way to Xenia and from there to New York. Craig's car. And the hot rod—Bill Piersall's car. And now the bulky Pontiac. And she did not even know to whom it belonged.

If I stayed out of cars, she thought oddly, I might stay out of trouble. But if I stayed out of trouble I wouldn't be April North, because April North seems to be nothing but a brainless blob who has one ever-loving hell of a knack for getting into trouble, not out.

Well, she was going to get out of trouble. She had made some mistakes, and Danny Duncan had been the first one, and Craig Jeffers had been an even worse one. For a while—a week, not much longer than that—she had thought herself in love with him. But any feeling she might have had for him was over. He had killed it.

Love? Not love, she knew. Sex, more than anything else. He had made her hear bells ring and rockets whistle, but the bells and the rockets were not signs of love. They were the fruits of sex. He was an expert, polished and accomplished, and he was able to lead her to heights of which she had never even dreamed.

But this hardly made them soulmates. Frank Evans had told her that sooner or later she would find out that Craig was a failure himself, just like everyone else at the party. And Frank Evans was right. Craig was dissipated and depraved, the same as Ken Rutherford who drank too much and the insatiably promiscuous Sue Maynor. Craig needed to try new kicks, new women, and he was incapable of love. He was rotten to the core. And she did not love him.

She rolled down the Pontiac's window and filled her lungs with night air. Tonight, she thought, she was getting rid of him forever. She was going to return the Pontiac and she was going to explain that she did not want to see him again, that she knew him for what he was and that obviously he was not for her. He probably would not mind too much, as far as it went. She was just a toy as far as he was concerned, that he had had his fun with. Probably he would be almost as glad to get rid of her as she was to get rid of him.

And after that? Nothing too glamorous, she thought. She'd already messed herself up by trying to turn herself into a glamor gal, darling of the suave set. And it had not worked at all. Deep down inside she was little April North, the daughter of an Antrim druggist. A month ago she'd been a virgin. And, while she could hardly grow back her virginity, she could do the next best thing. She could start being April North again.

She would live at home, with parents and brother. She would go to school, study diligently, and get the best grades she could possibly get. And she would live out the remainder of her senior year at Antrim High in a sort of social cocoon, turning down dates, avoiding other girls, and keeping to herself. She did not want to trade sex with Craig and his friends for sex with boys like Dan Duncan and Bill Piersall and Jim Bregger—that was no solution. She wanted to renounce sex entirely and start being a good girl all over again.

The rest of the year would be tough to get through.

She had a reputation, of course but the reputation would atrophy in time. And she could ignore the knowing glances easily enough, much as she had been ignoring them all week in school. After awhile they would tire of making remarks and passes.

And once she had graduated, everything would be simpler. She would go away to school—either land a scholarship or convince her father to spend an outrageous sum for her education. A bad reputation would not follow her across state lines.

College would give her a fresh start. She would still have a family to come home to, and this would be much better than her original idea of running away to New York. She would have a chance to mature at her natural pace, a chance to meet the right kind of guy and marry him and move to the right kind of town and have kids and be a good person.

She sighed. Craig's house was on her right, a few lights on downstairs. His Mercedes was parked in front. The other cars which had lain dormant there when she had left were gone. She pulled the Pontiac over to the side of the road, cut the engine, hauled on the emergency brake and got out of the car.

She rang Craig's doorbell and he let her in.

"Well," he said. "The little auto thief has returned."

"I didn't steal the car. I borrowed it."

He raised his eyebrows. "Ah, my dear. Do I detect a note of hostility in your words?"

"You're very perceptive."

"Is something wrong?"

"Something's wrong," she said. "Last night was just a little too much for me, Craig. Maybe I'm not as smooth and sophisticated as the girls you're used to. I don't care."

He slapped his hand to his brow in mock horror. "April," he said. "April, April, April. Come in, girl. Seat yourself, relax. You're all unnerved."

"I'm mad."

"Sit down, whatever you are. Would you like a drink?"

"No."

"A cigarette?"

"No."

"A session in bed?"'

She colored. "No," she said firmly.

"Then what do you want, April? Other than to return Sue's car. Frank Evans had to drive the poor lass home, and she wants her car back as soon as possible. Rather uncouth of you to take it, wouldn't you say?"

"I had to get home."

"You could have asked for a ride."

"You were sleeping," she said. "I didn't want to wake you."

"I wouldn't have minded."

"You were sleeping with a blonde. I didn't even want to stay in the same room with the two of you."

He laughed happily. "Wonderful! You're jealous, little girl. A rather bourgeois sentiment, but not without its own sort of merit. Actually you don't have to be jealous. The girl is unimportant enough. But she has the largest breasts I ever saw in my life. I simply had to find out what it was like to make love to a cow."

She drew a breath. "Well?"

"Well what?"

"How was it?"

"Interesting," he said.

"I'm glad you had an interesting time, Craig. And I'm not jealous. Not jealous of your blonde cow and not jealous of Sue Maynor."

She was angry, now, angry at him for what he was and at herself for not seeing through him sooner, for being blind to all the rotten streaks in the man. He was depraved and rotten from top to bottom, and she was sick at herself for ever having anything whatsoever to do with him.

"I'm not jealous," she went on. "I suppose I was, for a little while. But now I'm only revolted. I'm sick of you, Craig. You've got carloads of money and plenty of sophistication and you're nothing but a bum underneath it all."

"Really, April. A bum?"

"A bum. A horrible person—that's all you ever have been and all you ever will be. And I'm through with you, Craig. I'm through with this whole little life you and your friends have. It's not for me, not ever."

He stood up, walked to the wall, flicked a switch. Mood music filtered through the room. More props, she thought. Like the car and the house and the oh-so-dashing mustache. If you took away his props he was nothing at all.

"What life is for you, April?"

"A normal life."

"And what does that mean, pray tell?"

"A decent life," she snapped. "A life at home with my parents. Oh, you would call it a dull life, but it's the right way, Craig. I'll finish school at Antrim and I'll stay decent and I'll go away to college. It may sound commonplace but it's what I want."

He sighed. "You know," he said thoughtfully, "I thought you might feel something along these lines. And the thought of you going home to mama is more offensive than I can possibly tell you. So I've ruled out that course of action, girl."

"What are you talking about?"

He shrugged. "It should be clear enough," he said. "I mean exactly what I've just finished saying. You can't go home to the bosom of your revolting family. They'll throw you out on your ear."

"Why should they?"

"Because you're a slut," he said dispassionately. "Mind you, I'm not making a value judgment. Those are not my values, not by any means. But, in the eyes of your fatheaded father and your moronic mother, you are a slut."

She got to her feet. "I don't get it, Craig. Say what you mean."

"I'll do better than that. I'll show you."

She stood in her tracks while he walked across the room to a table. He opened a drawer and drew forth an envelope. Then he crossed the room again and presented the envelope to her with a flourish.

"Here you are," he said. "See for yourself."

She opened the envelope and nearly fell to the floor. As it was she took two steps backward and sat down again on the couch, her mouth open and her eyes wide.

"Go ahead," he said. "Look them over. Some of them are works of art, girl."

They were pictures. A dozen pictures, all told, and not one of them printable. And in each picture a young girl was plainly visible.

The girl was April North.

"How did you—"

"Take the pictures?" He grinned. "It was easy enough, my dear. Long ago I realized the advantage of candid photography. I've taken the trouble to install a camera or two in the walls of my bedroom. The expense was considerable, but I think you'll agree the results justify it. All that was required was to snap a remote control unit at the proper moment. I've taken dozens of pictures of you, April. These are the choicest items in the lot. They are nice, wouldn't you say?"

They were magnificent. A shot of her and Craig, she lying on her back, Craig between her white thighs. A shot of herself leaning face-down over the bed, feet on the floor, with Craig standing behind her.

A shot that showed only her face, catching her in an act which Craig had assured her was "perfectly natural," and which now made her want to vomit.

Another shot.

And more.

And, finally, a picture that had been taken the night before, in the garden. A picture of two female bodies intertwined on a terrycloth-covered chaise. One was the body of April North.

"Yes," he said, indicating the picture, "that one was rather a surprise. I was wandering in the garden and came upon you two, you and the redoubtable Margo. You were too excited to take notice of me, I'm afraid. So I scurried off for my camera and rendered the moment immortal. You know, you've rather a nerve to criticize me. You were having quite a time with Margo, girl."

"I was drunk."

"But hardly too drunk to enjoy yourself. Don't moralize in my direction, April. On the one hand you try to call yourself a free spirit, a sinless wonder. And on the other hand you castigate me for a lack of fidelity to you. A rather illogical position, wouldn't you say?"

She said nothing. He grinned again, pointing to the pictures. "And now you want to leave me, to flee to your family and live the good life again. Fortunately, you cannot do this. I've protected you from that, April."

"How?"

"With those pictures," he said. "Those art studies. Do you think your parents will welcome you when they've seen them?"

"They won't see them."

"But they will, dear."

She snatched the photographs, shredded them viciously. She tore each one in half and tore the halves in half while he watched her with a gleam in his eye.

"An empty gesture, April."

"Craig—"

He spread his hands, palms raised. "Your parents will see the photographs," he said. "It's out of my hands, really. This afternoon it occurred to me that you ought to bid your mother and father good-bye and move in with me on a permanent basis. To further that aim I sent a set of prints to your parents. I doubt that they'll receive you with open arms."

"You—"

"Mailed the pictures," he supplied. "That's exactly what I did. While I dropped dear Sweet Sue at her home in Xenia, I mailed the photographs. Your parents should receive them in the morning mail."

"I'll get them first."

"By staying home from school, April?"

"If I have to."

He sighed. "Not even that way," he said. "You see, I made up two sets of prints. I mailed one to your mother at your house. I dispatched the other to your father, the droll druggist, at his place of business. I don't think you'll be able to cut off both letters, dear April. Will you?"

She closed her eyes and thought that she was going to die. Everything, her future, her life, was wrecked, irreparably smashed, she knew. The pictures would kill whatever chance she might have had for happiness. There was no going back now, no living in her father's house, no life in Antrim.

It was over.

Over and done with.

Everything had seemed so simple before. Just get rid of Craig, go home, relax. Start living like a decent girl again, and in time everything would be all right.

Yes, she thought. That was the way she had worked out her

plans. But the future was not going to play itself out that way. A good decent future would have been nice, but a dozen filthy pictures showing April North having sex would make all that quite impossible.

"Damn you," she said.

He laughed.

"Damn you to hell. I hate you, Craig. I'd love to kill you. I'd like to cut your throat and watch you bleed."

"Do you hate me that much?"

"God, how I hate you." She turned from him, unable to look at him now. "You've ruined everything," she told him. "I had a chance until you sent those pictures out. I had a chance. I could have carved out a decent life for myself."

"You'd have died of boredom."

"I'd have been clean."

"Clean and dull. April, you've come a long way in a short time. You were beginning to learn what being a woman meant. Not a kitchen drudge like your mother—a real woman."

"I'd rather be a decent human being."

"You can't now, can you?"

She drew a breath. "No," she said, "I guess not. I guess you fixed everything, Craig."

He smiled at her. "You can move in here, you know."

"What!"

"You can move in with me," he repeated. "You can't go home, obviously. It's out of my hands and into the hands of the United States Post Office, and their hands are too strong for us to tamper with. But you can move into my house and share my bed and live the sort of life you've tasted recently. A good life, April. A wild free life that doesn't take a human being and turn him into a robot."

"With sex and parties?"

"With sex and parties," he said. "And don't try to make a saint out of yourself, child. You happen to like sex and parties. You happen to like everything about them. Don't deny it. You've loved everything I've given you and I've given you plenty. If you've got a brain in your feathery little head you'll move in here and like it. And sleep with anyone who asks you and have yourself a ball before you're dead."

Their eyes met, and she stared at him and let him stare at her. Then he dropped his eyes.

"No," she said.

"Are you certain?"

"Yes."

And her certainty must have showed because after a moment he simply shrugged and nodded his head. He told her she was making a mistake, and she said that she was not, that her greatest mistake had been Craig Jeffers.

"Then you're going?"

"Yes," she said.

"Can I give you a lift?"

"I'll walk."

"It's a long walk, April. And it's starting to rain outside. You'll get wet."

"I don't care."

"I see. Where are you going, April?"

"I don't know," she said. "Maybe New York. But it doesn't really matter, Craig. Nothing matters."

She started to the door. He moved to open it for her but she brushed him aside and opened it herself. He was right, rain had started and the night was gloomy. Soon she would get soaked.

But she did not care.

"April?"

"Go on."

"You should stay. You're doing something silly."

"No," she said. "I'm doing something smart."

She was halfway out the door when something occurred to her and she turned around, coming back inside the house. He was at the bar pouring himself a drink. He raised his eyes at her approach.

"Craig," she said, "before I said I'd love to kill you. But I don't wish you were dead."

"That's nice of you."

"I want you to live a long time," she said. "I don't want you to die young. I want you to live hard and fast, just the way you've always lived, without any moral code and without any sense of obligation to the rest of the world."

He said nothing.

"I want you to grow to be a very old man," she said. "Do you know why?"

"Why?"

"Because you'll be the saddest old man in the world," she said. "The most miserable old man in the whole world. You'd be very lucky if you died young, Craig, before you were old enough to see what a mess you were. And I don't want that to happen. I want you to live long enough to be wretched."

She walked out of the house and slammed the door and started walking.

She barely noticed the rain.

There was a lot of rain, and it was wet. In autumn Antrim has rainy days, and on these days it rains in spades. The sky opens up and the rain comes down, first in a drizzle and then in a torrent, and if you stay outside in the rain you get soaked through, despite galoshes, rainwear, umbrellas.

April had none of these. She was more than soaked. And she did not care.

No cars passed her in either direction while she walked down the narrow road from Craig Jeffers' house to Route 68. There was only the road and the trees at either side, only the wet and the damp, only the wind like a sword through silk. She was wearing dungarees and a sweater, the wholesome costume of the wholesome girl, and the dungarees and sweater were plastered against her body by the rain.

She went on walking.

There was no place to go now. No place to go and nothing to do. She was stuck. By tomorrow morning both her mother and her father would know that she was a tramp. A rumor alone they might have sloughed off, but a rumor and a photograph are two different things entirely. Quite probably the pictures would literally kill them. And if they did not have heart attacks over the photographs, they would still be killed on the inside.

And they would be through with her. That much was painfully obvious. She could never live with them again, or see them again, or think of them again as people close to her. Home was the place where, when you had to go there, they had to take you in. But she did not have to go there. And if she did, it would be too damned bad for April North, because after her parents saw the pictures they would not feel compelled to take her in.

She kept walking. She could go to New York, maybe. But she had no money, and she did not want to go home and pack a suitcase. And there was more to it than that. She could never feel right simply by running away, simply by escaping. There had been a time when that course had made sense but it did not make sense now.

Nothing did.

Maybe she could kill herself. It would not be difficult, she thought. Just run in front of a fast car, or lie down on a railroad track, or find a bridge and jump from it Maybe that was the logical answer. If there was nothing to look forward to but misery, what was the sense in staying alive?

No.

No, suicide was no answer. Suicide was ridiculous, because there was always some chance for happiness even if you could not see it at the moment. There was nothing to gain and everything to lose in giving up the gift of life.

No suicide.

Then what?

She reached 68 and started off away from Antrim and toward Xenia. She was walking away from Antrim rather than toward Xenia—God knew that there was nothing worth going to Xenia for, but she surely did not want to go home. She kept walking and wondering and then the car pulled up beside her.

At first she thought it was Craig. But it was not a Mercedes, not by any means.

And then she laughed.

Because she had come full circle, in some mysterious way, and the car beside her was a green Oldsmobile a year old, the green Oldsmobile where her virginity had been taken away in the back seat.

The driver was Danny Duncan.

CHAPTER 11

She was sitting at Danny's side in the front seat of the green Olds. She was not sure why she had entered the car but it had seemed like the right thing at the time. She was cold and drenching wet and shivering, and this particular car was where her trouble had all started, and somehow it seemed only fitting for her to get into the Olds now.

He had the radio playing rock-and-roll, and someone was singing *Get out the papers and the trash/Or you don't get no spending cash.* She tried not to listen to the blare of the radio, tried not to notice the huge raindrops splattering on the window.

"I shouldn't be here," she said.

"Why not, April?"

"Because you were rotten to me," she said.

"What do you mean?"

"You made love to me," she said. "And then you told all your friends about it. That wasn't very nice, Danny."

He looked sheepish.

"I hated you for a while," she went on. "But now I'm getting tired of hating people. I'm sick of it. There are too many rotten men in the world and if I keep on this way I'll hate all of them. I guess there's no future in it."

They rode a mile or so in silence. She looked across at him, at the handsome profile, the basketball build. She remembered that first time—strange, she thought, that it should seem so long ago.

"What's the trouble, April?"

"Everything's the trouble."

"Tell me about it. Maybe I can help."

She hesitated but only for a moment or two. "I have to go away," she said ultimately. "I have to leave Antrim."

"For good?"

"For better or for worse. If you mean forever, yes. I have to leave and I can't come back."

"Why?"

She looked at him. "I'm sorry," she said slowly, "but I'd rather not tell you."

"I can keep a secret."

"So I've noticed," she said bitterly. "Let's just say I have to leave town and let it lie there."

"Where will you go?"

"I don't know. New York, I guess."

"You'll take a train?"

"I guess. I don't have any money."

She had money, of course. She had the five hundred forty-three dollars and seventy-four cents that she had drawn from her savings account when she tried to leave Antrim for the first time. But that money was at home, safely tucked away, and she could not get it without going home.

And she could not go home.

"I don't have any money," she repeated.

He looked at her. The radio had shifted gears to a jolly little number called *Ave Maria Rock*. The rain was still coming down hard and fast. She felt his eyes brush over her body, noting how the wet sweater clung to her full breasts. She wished he would stop looking at her that way. She didn't like it, at all.

"Look, April. Maybe I can help."

He could have helped once, she thought. He could have been more of a man and less of a boy. He could have kept her secret in the first place, could have gone on loving her instead of permitting his love to be killed by her final acceptance of it. Then what would have happened? She might have married him, she thought—and she was suddenly glad that he had talked about her, because she could imagine very few ways to spend her life that were worse than as the wife of Danny Duncan.

"Just leave everything to me," he said. "You're going to have clean clothes and a hundred bucks, and then I'll drive you to Xenia and you can catch a night train to New York. You don't have a thing to worry about, April I'll take care of everything."

He was turning the car around now. He drove a mile on 68, then turned off onto a winding dirt road. The car splashed water from puddles in the middle of the road.

"Got to find a place for you to stay," he said. "While I go find those clothes for you."

"Where will you get them?"

"My sister," he said. "She's about your size and she won't miss a few clothes. I'll get the clothes and the money and come back for you. Meanwhile I know a place where you can stay."

"Where?"

"A barn. There's an old barn along this road—we used to hack around out here when we were kids. Nobody'll bother you. Hell, nobody ever goes there any more. You can relax and dry off while I get the clothes and the money."

"The money," she said.

"Yeah. A hundred dollars. That'll be enough for you, won't it?"

"Of course. But where will you get it?"

He chucked her under the chin. "Don't you worry about a thing," he said confidently. "I've got a pretty good idea where I'll get it. Don't worry, April."

The barn was old and sagging, weather-beaten and ready to crumble. But it was better on the inside than out. First of all, the interior was dry. Although the roof leaked in a dozen or more spots, there was one huge section where no rain dripped through, and that section was comfortable enough. The floor was covered with hay and dead leaves. The barn had a barnlike smell which she did not find unpleasant. This was certainly a hell of a lot better than wandering around in the rain.

"You'll be okay here," Danny said. Sure.

He was looking at her now, his eyes warm. She saw how he was staring at her breasts and she knew what was on his mind. He was not exactly hard to figure out.

"All this hay," he said. "Sort of a shame to let a place like this go to waste."

"Is that what you did when you used to come here?"

"We were just kids then," he said. "But now things are a little different."

She did not want to make love with him. She did not want to

make love with anybody, Danny Duncan least of all. She wanted, in fact, only to be away from Antrim and on her way to New York. But he was getting her dry clothes, was giving her a hundred dollars, and was driving her to Xenia—perhaps he deserved something in return. And she had only one thing to give.

So she offered no resistance when he came to her, taking her in his arms and pressing his mouth against hers in a kiss. At first she merely stood still like a robot, but then she realized that she might as well make it good, that he had probably never had a very experienced girl and that she could give him something he would never forget.

She ground against him, her loins seeking his, her mouth hot and demanding. She felt nothing, nothing at all, but her lack of feeling he would never have to know about. She would make it good for him. He let her go and stepped back. She looked at him, at the strong athlete's body. She felt no burst of passion, no rush of desire. In a sense, she was entirely cold-blooded about what she was going to do.

"Now, Danny."

He came to her again, embraced her, and they tumbled to the floor. She felt leaves and hay under her body, pricking her flesh a little, getting her itchy. She drew him down upon her and burned his mouth with a kiss. He was hotter than a two-dollar pistol now, she thought, and she herself was cooler and more accomplished than a two-dollar whore. Her tongue was in his mouth, doing wonderful things and driving him wild, and he was squirming on top of her, writhing with excitement.

He moved, his hands grabbing for her breasts. He squeezed the mounds of flesh, stroked them, patted them. She felt nothing, but she knew enough to feign excitement. She wriggled on the hay carpet, thrusting up her hips and softly moaning.

"You're the greatest, April. I never saw anybody like you. Never!"

She took one of his hands from her breast and moved it downward slowly, over her flat stomach. He touched her with greedy fingers, and she went on with her pantomime of passion, squirming and moaning as if his actions were exciting to her.

She thrashed beneath him, taking up the rhythm of love with the intensity of a dynamo, driving him outward and upward, making him moan and shriek with passion unlike anything he had ever experienced before. He bit her shoulder, cried her name to the skies.

Then he finished.

She held him for a moment, thinking that he was a child and that she was an old and sinful woman. She remembered the woman in Marseilles that Craig had talked about. Give me another twenty years, April North thought.

He got up slowly, his face flushed, his eyes wide. "That was—pretty great," he said.

"I'm glad you liked it."

He took a deep breath, held on to it for a moment, then let it out slowly. "I'd better get dressed," he said. "Better get going. So I can get the clothes and the money for you."

"Leave some cigarettes," she said.

"Sure."

"And some matches."

"Yeah, I will."

"And hurry back," she said.

•   •   •

She did not bother to get dressed. The clothes were wet and to put them on again would have been ridiculous. Instead she sat on a pile of loose hay and smoked three cigarettes one after the other. She did not think about anything in particular at the beginning. She merely sat on the pile of hay—which tickled her rear end slightly—and smoked the cigarettes. She put them out carefully. It would not do if the whole barn went up in a sheet of flame. People would be annoyed.

The time with Danny, she reflected, had been sort of interesting. It had done nothing to her, despite the incredible effect it had had upon him. The interesting part was the way she could turn on all her passion and still not feel a thing. Maybe that was the secret of a prostitute, she thought. Give the man his money's worth without losing any of your reserve. A valuable talent, no doubt. If everything went wrong in New York as it had gone so irremediably wrong in Antrim, she could always cash in on her ultimate negotiable asset and become a prostitute. She evidently had a bent for it

No, she thought. No, Danny Duncan had been the first and Danny Duncan would be the last. She was going to be good from here on out. She was going to get out of town, start fresh somewhere else, and this time everything would work itself out. She sat naked, smoking, letting her wet skin dry as the cool air hit it, and she waited for Danny to come back with clothes and money.

She heard a car and sprang to her feet. The car braked, and she ran to the door, keeping her naked body hidden and craning her neck to see who had arrived.

Not one car.

Five cars.

Each car stopped in turn. Doors flew open and boys piled out. About twenty of them, all with excited glints in their eyes and funny expressions on their faces. She recognized most of them; they were classmates at Antrim High, members of the senior class. She saw Jim Bregger, the fat pimply kid who had tried to date her when Danny had declared open season on April North. She saw other boys, and all of them were coming toward the barn.

Danny was leading them.

The rest waited outside. Danny came on in, and April stared at him. He tossed her a bundle of clothes—a wool plaid skirt, a yellow sweater, underwear and socks and shoes.

"Here you go," he said. "But don't put 'em on yet, April."

She did not understand.

"You need more than clothes," he went on. "You need money, too. A hundred bucks worth. Remember?"

She nodded.

"Well," he said, "I got the dough for you. A hundred bucks. See?"

He took a roll of five-dollar bills from his pocket and spread them before her in a fan. Then he folded them once and returned them to his pocket.

"A hundred bucks," he said. "All for you, April. All you have to do is earn it."

"I don't understand."

"Don't you?"

She shook her head. But actually she was afraid that she did understand, that she understood all too well. Her earlier thoughts—that she could always become a prostitute if everything else failed—came back to torment her. Apparently she was going to become a prostitute already.

"I didn't have a hundred bucks lying around, April. Hell, none of the guys have that kind of dough. But I found twenty guys with five bucks each. Five times twenty is a hundred, April. All you have to do is give each guy his five bucks worth and you'll have a hundred for yourself." He winked at her. "Judging from what I got a few minutes ago, it shouldn't be hard for you. Hell, let's face it. You're the hottest stuff around. You'll love every minute of it."

She wanted to tell him that she had only been pretending, that she would not love it at all. And she did not need the money, not really. It would be definitely easier to go home and get the money than to earn it by lying in a pile of hay while one boy after the other took his pleasure with her.

But what was the use? She was in a spot now. There were twenty boys outside, and they had not come out in the rain just to be turned down. If she tried to call the whole show off, she had a fairly good idea what would happen.

They would force her.

That would not be hard for them. They would hit her, and they would hold her down, and instead of a simple line-up it would be mass rape. Then they would not even give her the rotten hundred dollars—they would leave her half-dead in the barn and go away.

"Suppose I don't want to," she said, feeling him out.

"You've got to."

"And if I won't?"

"You will."

The certainty with which he said those two words convinced

her that she was right. She had no chance. She looked at him, looked at the cocky expression on his face, and she knew that he was not going to let this opportunity slip through his fingers. She was stuck.

"You're quite an organizer," she told Danny. *Quite a pimp,* she silently amended.

He took her words for a compliment. "It was nothing," he said modestly. "All I had to do was pass the idea around. Everybody went for it like a shot."

"They did?"

"Sure," he said. "Everybody's pretty darn hot to get to you, April. They're panting all over the place. Every guy I asked was off like a shot to pick up five bucks and come after you. Some of them went and borrowed the dough."

It was almost funny.

"All except Bill Piersall," he went on. "You know, the jerk took a poke at me when I mentioned the deal to him."

"He did?"

"Yeah. Jesus, I wanted to powder him. Here I was, letting him in on a good deal, and he started yelling that I should leave you alone, that you were a decent girl and I was a son of a bitch. He's a real farmer, let me tell you. Sticking up for you like a clown. He can't realize that you just love to get it night and day."

She wanted to laugh, then changed her mind and wanted to cry. All along Bill had been sticking up for her, trying to treat her as a decent girl, while she was playing harlot for Craig Jeffers. And Bill was the one she'd vented all her anger on, the one she had brushed off repeatedly.

"He's some kind of a nut," Danny said.

A nut? Maybe, she thought. He must be nuts if he likes me. But he did like her, liked her and respected her in spite of what she had done. And it was not as if he were an innocent kid with a distorted picture of a girl named April North. She could still remember the time he had made love to her in the woods, and she knew how good it had been, better than she had ever permitted herself to realize.

Bill was not after sex. He had had that, and he wanted more. He wanted her—as a person, as a girl, as a woman. But it was too late now.

Too late. Because what might have been could never be now, and whatever chance she had had for happiness with Bill was shot to hell and gone. Now she would turn her tricks for Danny and his boys and take her hundred dollars and run. If she did not, she would just be stuck all over again. Danny would probably take back the clothes and leave her high and dry—or more accurately, low and damp. She would miss out on the ride to Xenia and the money and the dry clothes, and she would probably spend the rest of her life in the abandoned barn waiting for the rain to stop. "Want to get started, April?"

She looked at him. For a second she glared, and he flinched from the venomous hatred her eyes revealed. But instantly she masked this expression and flashed what was supposed to be a coy smile. "I'm ready," she said.

He laughed, turned and went outside. She waited, inwardly sick, until the first boy came in. She recognized him but could not remember his name. He was tall and gangling, with nervous eyes that could not quite meet hers and at the same time could not stay away from her ripe body. He stared at her legs and breasts and his tongue was hanging out.

A virgin, she thought. A simple slob who didn't know what a woman was like. "Well," she said. "I won't bite." He stammered something unintelligible. "Get those silly clothes off," she said.

I'm old and jaded, she thought. *What's the difference? It all makes no difference.*

But the gangling boy never got to her. There was noise in the background, a car pulling up sharply, a door opening and banging shut. And then the boys out front were yelling, and then a man was bursting through the open door of the barn.

Craig.

"You stupid urchin," he yelled at the boy. "Get away from her, you fool!"

The boy backed away, confused. Craig charged into the room and swung a fist at the boy. The boy caught the punch with the tip of his chin and went down as though pole-axed. He fell to the floor and did not move.

Craig turned to April, his eyes bright. "Well, how lovely," he said, lips curling in a smile. "This is the reformation of April North, isn't it? I looked all over for you, dear. I wondered what had happened to you. And then I passed a caravan of cars loaded with boys singing dirty songs. And sure enough, dear, they led me straight to you."

She tried to cover her nakedness with her hands and he laughed at her.

"April North's life of purity," he said. "Taking on the senior class. What are they paying you, April?"

"One hundred dollars."

"Great Caesar's ghost," he said. "That's magnificent. Get your clothes on, April. If you've got to play harlot, you might as well do it properly. You can live a life of luxury for the same work."

"With you?"

"With me. It's only sensible, April. If you're going to use sex to stay alive, you might as well get some benefit out of it. You'll live luxuriously at my house. You'll have parties and friends and excitement instead of serving as a doormat for the students of Antrim High School. Doesn't it make a little more sense that way, dear?"

It did. She had sworn to stay away from Craig, but now she was only selling herself cheaply. If she had to be a tramp, she might as well make it pay. And it would pay better as Craig's mistress than as mistress for twenty kids, all of them damp behind their ears.

Danny was in the doorway, shouting something, yelling at Craig. She saw Craig step in close to him, then lash out with his right foot. Danny buckled, clapping his hands to his groin and groaning, his face contorted with pain. The edge of Craig's hand came down in a deadly chop and caught Danny on the side of the throat. The boy fell all the way down, landing in a crumpled heap on the barn floor.

"Get dressed," Craig snapped. "These churls won't bother us. They have us outnumbered, but that won't do them any good."

She dressed quickly, putting on the clean dry clothes Danny had gotten from his sister. April tried not to look at Craig while she dressed. She felt terrible, but there was nothing else for her to do. She had had one chance—Bill Piersall—but she had muffed it. And you did not get a second chance. "Come on," Craig said.

They were in the Mercedes now. The other boys were milling

around, trying to get up the courage to try to get their prize away from Craig. But they did not have enough time. Craig started the sleek sports car and spun around in a fast U-turn, heading back toward 68. He put the accelerator on the floor and the car was a streak in the night.

April noticed another noise, another car spinning around in a tight U-turn and coming after them. She looked over her shoulder, and her heart leaped up into her throat and she could not swallow it down again. The car was a hot-rod. The driver was Bill Piersall.

CHAPTER 12

"Who," said Craig, "is that?"

She was still staring, open-mouthed in wonder. It's my knight in shining armor, she wanted to say, my knight on a charger of nuts and bolts.

She said: "It's Bill."

"Bill?"

"Bill Piersall," she said. "The boy who made his own hot-rod. I was telling you about him."

"And what's he doing?"

"Chasing us," she said.

Craig laughed. "Chasing a Mercedes in a home-made job? He must be out of his mind."

Craig had the accelerator on the floor but the rod was coming on in hot pursuit. They were pulling away from Bill, moving away, and she felt almost as though she were being torn in two. Because she realized all at once that she wanted Bill to catch them, to draw ahead of them and force the Mercedes to stop. Bill still loved her, she thought. He still wanted her.

"I'll show that whelp what a real car can do," Craig was saying. "Watch this, April."

She was watching the hot-rod instead. She thought of the way she had contrasted Bill and Craig by contrasting their cars. But she had had it all wrong, she knew now. Craig was a rich man's son who bought the car he wanted with money he had inherited. But Bill had built the car he wanted, had put it together with his own hands and his own sweat. Any rich man could buy a Mercedes and drive hell out of it. Not everyone could build a rod like Bill's.

And, amazingly, the rod was gaining on them. She stared at it, saw Bill at the wheel, concentrating on his driving with single-minded attention. He was pulling almost even with the Benz, his hands riveted to the steering wheel. It amazed her that a car so sloppy in appearance could be capable of such a burst of speed.

Well, appearances were deceiving. She had misjudged Bill's car just as she had misjudged Bill, and now she was just beginning to see the light when it was almost too late to do any good. They were careening down the dirt road now, the rod just a few feet behind the Mercedes, with Route 68 not far ahead.

"Dammit!" Craig was shouting. His face was flushed and the effort was telling on him. "That little bastard—"

Craig swerved sharply to his left, brushing the nose of the rod in an effort to spin the rod off the road. But Bill held on, sweeping to his left and putting on an extra burst of speed to draw even with the Mercedes. He went out in front, then slashed sharply across in front of the Benz. April saw the look of horror on Craig's face, saw the nose of the Benz moving toward the tail of the rod, and she knew they were going to crash.

The rod did it neatly. Bill tickled the Mercedes' nose, then spun forward. But Craig did not make it. The car careened out of control, spilling over the side of the road.

April held her breath . . .

•   •   •

She was thrown up over the side of the car and into a pile of brush at the side. Her arms and legs were scratched and her head ached but she was alive and more or less unhurt. She raised herself onto one elbow, and then she saw Bill.

His car was parked on the road ahead, miraculously unhurt. And Bill was at the Mercedes, working feverishly. He managed to lift the unconscious Craig, dragged him off to one side.

The Mercedes burst into flames, burning like a beacon at the roadside. The racy automobile was no longer a dream car, no longer a car at all—just flaming metal and leather.

She ran to Bill, calling his name.

Sweat coursed down his face. He lowered Craig into wet grass and stood for a moment, looking at him. He checked Craig's pulse, listened to his heart beat.

"He'll live," he said.

"Bill—"

"Are you all right, April?"

"I'm all right."

"Are you positive?"

"Yes," she said. "I'm positive."

"I wanted to tear Danny's head off," he said. "When he told me what he was setting up I blew my top. I wanted to take him apart and throw the parts away."

"He told me."

"I had to find you. He didn't tell me where he was keeping you and I started chasing around looking in likely spots. I remembered the barn and got here just when you and this jerk were pulling away." He sighed. "I guess I got here just in time, huh?"

She could say nothing. She looked at Bill, remembering the hurtful things she had said to him, and realizing how wrong she had been about him from the beginning. He was a good person, a fine person. He was not Danny Duncan and he was not Craig Jeffers.

He was something special.

"I'd better get you home," he said.

"I can't go home."

"Why not?"

Haltingly she told him about the pictures. At first she was sick with embarrassment, but as she talked she realized that she would never have to be embarrassed with Bill. He respected her; moreover, he was able to accept her for what she was and at the same time to honor her for what he felt she could be. She explained how impossible it would be for her to stay in Antrim.

"I can see that," Bill said. "You can't stay here. And neither can I, April."

"Why not?"

"Because I have to be where you are, April. I can't be alive unless I'm with you. See?"

"Bill—"

"I love you, April."

She started to say something but his mouth stopped her words before they could be spoken. All at once he was holding her, his hands damp with sweat, and he was kissing her, his mouth hard against hers. She did not love him. But love was not the most important consideration now.

He gave her an out. If Bill took care of her everything would be all right. She could stay with him, marry him if that was what he wanted, and she would be out of Antrim and safe somewhere else.

Would it be fair to him? It would, she told herself. She could be a good wife whether she loved him or not. She would be faithful and warm, and he would never know that she was not in love with him.

She stayed close to him. He smelled of sweat and axle-grease and masculinity, and she buried her face in his chest and hugged him as hard as she could.

"Come on," he said. "Let's get going, April."

"Where to?"

"I'll tell you on the way."

"What about—him?"

"The jerk with the Merc? To hell with him, April. He's alive. He'll get back home somehow. His kind always manage. They step on people and grind them into the dirt and they always come out of it smelling like a rose. You don't have to worry about him, April. He'll get along."

She followed Bill to the hot-rod. She sat next to him, and he started the rod down the road. He turned right on 68, heading toward Xenia and away from Antrim forever.

They sat at a table in the rear of the diner in Yarborough, a few miles east of the Indiana state line. The waitress brought four hamburgers and two cups of black coffee.

"Let's dig in," Bill said. "I'm starving."

She picked up a hamburger and began gnawing it. The meat tasted good—maybe not like a seven-course meal at Kardaman's, but just as good when you were hungry enough to appreciate it. She devoured the first hamburger, then took a sip of the steaming coffee and made a face.

"I know," he said. "This stuff tastes like battery acid. It's slop. But it'll help keep us awake. We've got to do a lot of driving tonight."

"Where are we going, Bill?"

"I'm not sure. Into Indiana, first of all. Maybe across Indiana and into southern Illinois."

"And what will we do there?"

"We'll get married," he said.

Married. No one else wanted to marry her, she remembered. Not Danny, not Craig. But Bill didn't even ask her if she wanted a wedding ring. He simply took it for granted that she would marry him.

That sounded wonderful.

"And then?"

He shrugged. "Then we find a little town," he said. "It doesn't have to be much, just a little place where we can live our own lives the way we want to. That's all we need, April. Just a place to live in and each other to live with."

"How will we stay alive?"

He put down his hamburger. "It won't be hard," he said. "I'm a damned good mechanic, April. I can do anything in the world with a car. And a top mechanic can always get a job. There's not a town in the world without a garage, and there are damn few garages that can't use a good hand. We'll find one that can and I'll have a job."

"I can work, too."

"You don't have to."

"But I want to," she said. "I can get a job waiting on tables or something like that."

"With truck-drivers making passes at you all day long? That doesn't sound too good."

"I'll manage," she said. "They won't make passes for long. Because it won't do them any good. When a girl is lucky enough to be married to the best man in the world, no truck driver is going to tempt her."

He smiled at her, reached across the small table to take her hand. He squeezed her hand and she thought that love was not so important after all. Whether or not she loved him, she was very lucky to have found him, to be with him. Together they could build a real life. A good life.

"We have to save money," she went on. "So we can buy a house and fill it with children."

"Do you want children, April?"

"I want your children."

"I love you, April."

"And I love you, Bill."

The lie came easily to her lips. She would have to repeat that lie for a lifetime, she knew. But she would never let him know that she did not love him. She had to make him very happy; she owed him that much and more.

She ate her second hamburger and smoked a cigarette while Bill got a second cup of coffee. She watched him drink the coffee.

When he finished it and set the empty cup back in the saucer, she grinned at him.

"You know," she said, "you can back out, if you want."

"Why should I want to?"

"Because you're getting second-hand goods."

"April—"

"I'm not exactly a virgin," she went on. "I've done some pretty disgusting things. I'm a mess, Bill. You're getting used goods and you don't have to get stuck with them."

"Maybe I want to."

"Still—"

His eyes were very serious. "You know my car, April?"

"Of course."

"It's a hell of a car," he said. "It can out-drag a Mercedes, you saw it do that. Funny thing about that car, April. It's just a bucket of bolts when you come right down to it. The body is off an old Ford that must have rusted to hell and gone twenty years ago. The transmission's off a LaSalle, and they haven't made LaSalles since before the second world war. The engine came out of a Chrysler that got knocked to hell in a wreck. Just a collection of broken-down parts."

She waited for him to go on. Instead he lit a cigarette and smoked for a few seconds. Words did not come easily to him; he was not as glib as Craig, but when he spoke he said what he meant and meant what he said. And this was far more important than glibness.

"If the parts are good," he said slowly, "it doesn't matter a hell of a lot how many wrecks the car's been in, or what kind of mileage it's carrying. I guess it's not flattering to compare you to an old car, April. But you get what I mean, don't you? I don't give a damn what you've done or who you did it with. All I care about is the kind of girl you are."

Craig would have spoken the words differently. He would have used an image far more poetic than a simple thing like a hotrod. But somehow Bill's words could not make her laugh, or even feel like laughing. She knew that he meant what he said, that his simple words were essentially far more poetic than the colorful lies Craig Jeffers had told her.

She could say nothing in reply. She wished suddenly that she did love him, knowing how much he deserved her love.

But she was not without feeling for him. He was good, he was sweet, he was gentle—and she liked him for these qualities. She liked the person he was, the fine person he was.

"Hell," he said. "I talk too much. Let's get out of here and put some miles on the rod."

The name of the town was Birch Creek.

The town was not so much. There were a few hundred less people than in Antrim, and the summers were a little warmer and the winters not so cold, and southern Illinois was not quite the same as southern Ohio. Aside from that, Birch Creek could have been Antrim all over again. And yet the town was entirely different.

April stood at Bill's side in the rectory of the small church while the minister said things to them, and when the minister finished saying things Bill put a five-dollar ring on her finger and took her in his arms.

"Some day I'll get you a better ring," he told her the night before. "A decent one, with diamonds."

But she had said, "This is all the ring I ever want. Just this and you. Who needs diamonds?"

So they were married in Birch Creek, and they took a two-room kitchenette apartment on the main street of town above a dry-goods store. They spent their wedding night in a motel three miles from town. Bill had said that you just could not spend your wedding night in your own home, and that the motel would be worth the five bucks it cost them.

It was worth more than that.

It was worth the world.

She learned something that night, something that made her want to laugh and cry at once. She had gone with Bill to get away from the town, to escape her problems and start in fresh. And a very strange thing had happened.

She had fallen in love with him.

This was love, she knew. This was love, and it made the cardboard infatuation with Craig fall away and disappear as if it had never existed in the first place. This was love, and she had been miraculously lucky, managing to get away from Antrim and at the same time finding love as an added dividend.

Because that night someone opened the gates to Heaven and the world went away in a shining pink cloud. That night it was not sex but love, not flesh but a pair of spirits meeting. Everything Bill did to her made her realize how lucky she was, how happy she was going to be.

"Your name is Mrs. Piersall now," he had said, his mouth close to her ears. "How does it sound?"

It sounded wonderful.

The lovemaking was gentle and fiery at once, a mutual meeting that words would only injure. It was fire and ice, softness and hardness, everything good and nothing bad. Bill was her husband, he had given her a ring, and now she was giving him a ring in return. It was perfection, utter perfection, and it washed away all the ugliness of her past.

The bad parts simply dissolved and disappeared. Danny Duncan was gone now. So was Craig Jeffers. And the night with Margo Long, the lesbian interlude conducted in horrid drunkenness on the chaise in Craig's garden, simply ceased to exist. It was as though it had never happened at all. There was only Bill, Bill her lover, Bill her husband, Bill her man.

Nothing else.

They would have a good life now. They were in a town that accepted them as a decent pair of newlyweds starting life together. Bill had a good job and she was working part-time in a restaurant. They were saving money, money for a home and children.

Sometimes she lay awake at night after Bill had dropped off to sleep and her mind wandered back to Antrim. She had almost lost Bill. She had come close to running to New York, had come even closer to ruining and wasting her life with Craig.

She had been very lucky.

And she lay in bed snug at Bill's side, listening to his measured breathing, and she thought about her luck. She had everything she had ever wanted now. She was going to hang onto it. She was going to stay happy forever.

She thought about the happiness that waited for them. The happiness of a house of their own, for example. The happiness of being parents, of having children. The happiness of growing old, not as Craig Jeffers would grow old, alone and bitter, but as two people aging together, side by side, always close, always in love.

She liked Birch Creek and she was incredibly happy there. But the town was immaterial. It might as well have been Cedar Hills or Brackle or Lipton's Landing. Any town would do.

The background didn't matter. She mattered, and Bill mattered, and that was all.

My Newsletter: I get out an email newsletter at unpredictable intervals, but rarely more often than every other week. I'll be happy to add you to the distribution list. A blank email to lawbloc@gmail.com with "newsletter" in the subject line will get you on the list, and a click of the "Unsubscribe" link will get you off it, should you ultimately decide you're happier without it.

Lawrence Block has been writing award-winning mystery and suspense fiction for half a century. You can read his thoughts about crime fiction and crime writers in *The Crime of Our Lives*, where this MWA Grand Master tells it straight. His most recent novels are *The Girl With the Deep Blue Eyes*; *The Burglar Who Counted the Spoons*, featuring Bernie Rhodenbarr; *Hit Me*, featuring Keller; and *A Drop of the Hard Stuff*, featuring Matthew Scudder, played by Liam Neeson in the film *A Walk Among the Tombstones*. Several of his other books have been filmed, although not terribly well. He's well known for his books for writers, including the classic *Telling Lies for Fun & Profit*, and *The Liar's Bible*. In addition to prose works, he has written episodic television (*Tilt!*) and the Wong Kar-wai film, *My Blueberry Nights*. He is a modest and humble fellow, although you would never guess as much from this biographical note.

Email: lawbloc@gmail.com
Twitter: @LawrenceBlock
Facebook: lawrence.block
Website: lawrenceblock.com